Blood from a Stone

a selection of new writing

Edited by Sofie Baekdal,
Bruce Johns, James Kennedy
and David Wake

Published by **Imprimata**
for and on behalf of The School of English, Birmingham City University.

First published 2012
Compilation © The School of English,
Birmingham City University 2012
Contributions © individual copyright holders

The School of English, Birmingham City University has asserted its rights under the Copyright Designs and Patents Act 1988 to be identified as the author of this compilation.
All rights reserved. No part of this publication may be reproduced, stored in or introduced into a retrieval system, or transmitted in any form or by any means, (electronic, mechanical, photocopying, recording or otherwise, and whether invented now or subsequently) without the prior written permission of The School of English, Birmingham City University, or be otherwise circulated in any form, other than that in which it is published, without a similar condition being imposed on any subsequent publisher.
Any person who does any unauthorized act in relation to this publication may be liable to criminal prosecution and civil action.

A CIP Catalogue record for this book is available
from the British library

ISBN 978-1-906192-69-3

Designed and typeset in Chaparral Pro with InDCS5.5
by Mark Bracey @ Imprimata

Printed in Great Britain

Imprimata

An imprint of InXmedia Limited
www.imprimata.co.uk

Contents

Foreword by Ian Marchant

Diffraction by Oliver Balp	PROSE	3
One is One and All Alone by Michèle Barzey	PROSE	13
Train Untrained or Derailed No. 15 by Ted Bonham	POETRY	19
You're Going to be in Trouble by Adam Brett	PROSE	23
The Mermaid Tank by Richard Burke	PROSE	33
New York 1985 by Michael B. Cahill	PROSE	35
Sit Down and Talk by Tom Clements	PROSE	41
Lardy Lee's Revenge by Paul Costello	PROSE	45
Turtles for Christmas by Rebekah Dunne	PROSE	59
Bittersweet by Georgina Shackell Green	POETRY	75
Inside by Cherrelle Higgs	PLAY	77
Untitled by Ross Horton	POETRY	97
Mi Viejo by Francisco Iannuzzi	PROSE	99
Signore Bigshot by Bruce Johns	PROSE	107
Night Fishing by Derek Littlewood	POETRY	123
The Riparian by Kate Mascarenhas	SCREENPLAY	127
A Rat's Tale by Geoff Mills	PROSE	149
A Fairy Tale by Sheryl Prior	PROSE	161
Dance the Ghost with Me by Rhoda Thompson	PROSE	173
Hang up by David Wake	PROSE	175
The Bucket Hunt by Daniel Wilkes	PROSE	191
Collision by Suzanne Wright	PROSE	197

IAN MARCHANT is a writer, broadcaster and lecturer in Creative Writing at Birmingham City University.

He has published two novels and three volumes of travel memoir as well as writing features for *The Observer*, *The Telegraph*, *The Independent*, *The Times* and *Metro*, and op-ed for *The Times* and *The Sunday Express*. He was co-writer on *White Open Spaces* produced by Pentabus Theatre and BBC Radio Drama, which was nominated for a South Bank Show award in 2007. He has broadcast extensively for BBC Radio Three and Radio Four, and has presented several documentaries for ITV, one of which, *Telford*, was nominated for a Royal Television Society Award in 2008.

Between 1998 and 2000 he lived up a lane in a caravan, ate tinned sardines, and sat around fires in buckets.

His latest book, *Something of the Night*, is available from Simon & Schuster and the one after that, *A Hero for High Times*, is due for publication by Jonathan Cape in 2013.

Foreword
by Ian Marchant

Writing is one of the few human activities which gets harder the more you practise. I've been a practising writer for 25 years, and, where once upon a time vibrant apercus, elegant plot devices and sparkling dialogue leapt unbidden from my fingertips through the keyboard and onto the computer screen, nowadays I find I can sit for hours in front of my monitor thinking "What exactly do I mean by '*and*' in this sentence?" Writing is hard.

Thomas Mann said "A writer is someone who finds writing harder than other people," but I think he's over-stating it a bit, because otherwise, Wayne Rooney and Katie Price and their ilk wouldn't need ghosts, since, as non-writers, they would find it much easier to write than the writers they hire to ghost the stuff for them. Perhaps they never bothered trying. They never practised. Writing is hard, but only if you practise: like anything, I guess. Rooney practised football, and Katie Price practised vajazzling, both of which, I'm assured, need a great deal of heart-breaking effort to get anywhere near to being any good. Mann is an idiot, quite frankly. Anything is easy if you don't do it. Writing is easy. Re-writing, though, is the very devil.

The writers in this excellent anthology are all practising re-writers, and it has been a pleasure to help them with their practice as I struggle with my own. These writers have taught me much and reminded me of much more. They have reminded me of the power of the creative imagination, of the partial usefulness of rules, of the need to keep seeking out the thin ice. They have reminded me that writers must be brave, or nothing, because writing at its best, as in this collection, is always unsafe.

Blood from a Stone

OLIVER BALP is studying for a BA in English and Creative Writing and aims either to follow this with an MA or to escape immediately to foreign shores. He hopes to work in screenwriting if possible and has a particular passion for science fiction. Dr. Gregory Leadbetter described Oliver's humour in his recent radio play as being "at times a little too juvenile - even for me". He has won several school competitions, including a poetry prize for a piece wondering why Father Christmas was overweight. He has worked at the British Embassy in Abu Dhabi, as a waiter in a seedy seaside hotel and as an onsite investigator for Lankelma in Iden.

Diffraction
by Oliver Balp

4th November 1993

"Dad, why is Mummy screaming?"

A vague murmur sounded from the bed below me.

"Daddy! Dad! Is Mum OK?"

He stretched then lifted me off the top-bunk and put me down at his feet. Sleepily he ruffled my hair. We toddled to my parents' room across the hall, rubbing our eyes and feeling the walls like we were in a cartoon. Mum wasn't screaming when my Dad opened the door. There were people in white coats standing around her. She looked strange, smiling beneath her red eyes, while one of the ladies in white coats held a little pink lump in a towel.

"What's that?"

Dad was sitting down near Mum on the bed, holding her hand.

"That's your new baby sister."

This is my first memory. Esmé's first few moments in our family home in Hastings.

Before starting nursery at three years old, Esmé would stay with our Grandmother during the days our parents were at work. Using an innate cunning peculiar to toddlers she would exploit the morning schedules of our parents so that she could eat two breakfasts every weekday before she left the house. Following this manipulation she would somehow manage to arrive, hungry, at our Grandmother's for her third breakfast. I am only able to repeat this information after it was revealed in a chance conversation ten years later.

Shortly after Esmé turned three, our Mum decided to take her out on a shopping trip with her friend. She turned around for a 'split second' to look at a raincoat and Esmé disappeared. Our Mum locks her cat indoors every time the air visibility is anything other than perfect. She frenzied around the shop searching for her daughter. Upon request, the management called the police five minutes after Esmé initially went missing and found a chair for our Mum to take an edge of discomfort away from her fear and hyperventilation. Ten minutes after this, Esmé was found, observing the entire scene from behind a rail of coats.

At five years old, Esmé was overweight and starting primary school. She once remarked that this was an important time in her life because it taught her 'humility'. One morning our headteacher was giving us a speech about the importance of kindness to others. A blind man came up to the front of the hall to give a talk afterwards. He laid some props on a table at the front of the assembly hall. While he was talking, he gestured with his hands and knocked something off the table. The hall filled with children's laughter and seated teachers who lined the walls rose to hush them. Amid the commotion, Esmé got up and retrieved the prop before giving it back to the speaker.

Our family moved to the United Arab Emirates in November 2002. My sister cried on the plane in our mother's arms. She wailed the names of our Grandma and Auntie while our Mum stroked her hair and spoke to her in her most soothing voice. When we arrived, Mum's company put us up in a five-star hotel on the coast while we settled in. I asked if we could stay there forever. Esmé asked if she could go home.

Not used to homework in her previous school, Esmé was reluctant to tackle her workload for a few months when we began our studies in Al-Khubairat. Following this teething time however, something in the foreign air perhaps began to stir within her.

> "Acquire knowledge, it enables its professor to distinguish right from wrong; it lights the way to heaven. It is our friend in the desert, our company in solitude and companion when friendless. It guides us to happiness, it sustains us in misery, it is an ornament amongst friends and an armour against enemies."
>
> *Widely attributed to the Prophet Mohammed*

After two years in Abu Dhabi, Esmé was a straight-A student. My parents and I would struggle to drag her away from her studies so that she could attend birthday parties that had popcorn machines and goody bags with mobile phones in them. In the last year of primary school she decided to run for a position as either a prefect or head girl. I suggested that she should do something a little different for her presentation, so we stayed up late for four nights writing a soundtrack and rhyming the things that she wanted to change. After she stood up in front of the school and rapped her presentation, she got a standing ovation and an almost unanimous vote in her favour for both positions. The head teacher asked her which she would like and she chose to be head girl so that she could implement her policies, most of which were aimed at reducing bullying, which she did. The day after the presentation, to our Mum's surprise, a number of her colleagues approached her with congratulations on Esmé's performance. Her name is still on a plaque in Al Khubairat Primary School today.

At parents' evening that year the Islamic Studies tutor gave Esmé the honour of being the only non-Muslim pupil ever to be invited to take the subject in the history of the school - to our atheist Dad's mild disappointment. She declined the offer for reasons unknown, but would often read a variety of different religious texts in her spare time.

After five years in Abu Dhabi, we returned to our house in the UK. My sister and I each received a letter in the post from our headmaster. Mine was a short line that said "Oliver can be a good student, when he decides to be." Esmé's was too long to write down, but the phrase 'model student' was included more than once. It seemed like she was going to be the first Balp with a strong academic record, and our French Granddad, who remarked when my mother was pregnant with Esmé, "Si c'est une fille de le renvoyer" - "If it's a girl, send it back" - sent a long proud email to us after he read her report.

One night, while I was out chasing girls, Esmé sat with our Mum in the living room. She was fourteen years old.

"Mum, I think I might be asexual."

"Oh, I wouldn't worry about that. It's something that will come with time, I'm sure."

During her teenage years she was very prudish about certain things and would never say the word 'bra' in front of anyone, preferring the term 'thing'. She shed a lot of the puppy fat that she used to have as a child and quickly grew as tall as our Dad, though the latter is hardly any kind of achievement. Despite her age, she would always snap at us if we ever referred to her as a teenager, telling us she was still a child, and seemed oblivious to the irony of her angst. She started to attend Saint Richard's Catholic School while I was at college and quickly became the star member of the debating team and somewhat of an urban legend for her charming and argumentative nature in lessons. Her RE teacher told me she was the only pupil who ever said, "Well you're wrong, and now I'm going to tell you why." He wrote in her year book, "I know teachers aren't meant to have favourites, but …"

Apparently she was the only bus monitor (and senior prefect) who completely stopped bullying on the bus in the mornings. According to other pupils she made it look easy. One morning she saw a boy slap another student.

"You, sit on your hand," she said. His victim decided to kick him while he was disarmed.

"And you... sit on your foot."

She studied hard and achieved eight A* grades and 3 As in her GCSEs. Science was her favourite subject. When people asked her what she wanted to do in the future, she would often reply, "I want to find the cure for cancer," and when she saw me smoking she would say "Don't smoke, Ols. You're so thin that it really doesn't suit you."

Studying the necessary A-levels to become a medical doctor, she was disappointed at the sub-standard teaching standards in Bexhill College that I had relished two years earlier. Her grades were uncharacteristically low that year so Mum got her a personal tutor for the second semester and she received AAB grades in her mock re-takes.

In her second year of college, at eighteen years old, she did volunteer work at Bexhill Buddhist Centre and intermittently attended Catholic Mass on Sundays. Taking advantage of her non-genetic love of Christmas and children, she managed get a job at Lapland UK, snatching a specially written part from the clutches of postgraduate drama students. She was performing to two hundred people at a time in Lapland UK as her character the 'eco elf,' and decided that she didn't want to go straight to university after college, so applied to work in Disneyland, Florida, enchanted by the growing pull of distant horizons.

> "Conduct yourself in this world, as if you are here to stay forever; prepare for eternity as if you have to die tomorrow."
> *Bukhari*

As the petals of 2010 browned at the edges, Esmé started to go out after work and sit at band practice with a boy called Mike. He left college to work as a kitchen porter in a hotel and Mum noticed that Esmé had started to wear a plectrum he gave her. It was in the shape of a heart, and she wore it around her wrist on a red ribbon.

Once a boy called Callum Suppu came round to the house.
"Is this the one you were telling me about?" I asked
"Yes, it is."
"What's the matter?" he asked.
"Callum's a poo!" I exclaimed triumphantly. My girlfriend, Josie, and Esmé tried to calm me down while I keeled over laughing. Even that crushing embarrassment didn't foil him, and Mum said she heard her talking to Callum on the phone a few times after that. Esmé was never interested in him though, despite our constant hints at how rich he was.

On the 19th December 2011 Esmé put make-up on for the first time. Mum drove her to the train station, so she could go to a party. *I should really teach her how to put on eye-liner,* Mum thought but she didn't say anything because she knew it would make Esmé wipe it all off.

"Be careful and if you need anything, just call me. I love you."
"I love you too, Mum."

Later at the party she decided to have a few glasses of alcohol. This was the first time in two years because my sister and I both suffer from alcohol intolerance. It isn't too severe - it just gives us heartburn. She felt unwell so she went for a walk to Tesco with her friend. Mike offered to come along. They asked what people would like from the shop. As she had turned eighteen just over a month before the party it would be the first time she could buy alcohol. While they walked back Esmé was between her friend and Mike. Suddenly she stopped as they left Ravenside Retail Park.

"That's strange. Did you feel that?"
"Feel what?" said Mike.
"Look at that, my watch has stopped. I don't think I can go on." Her friends laughed.
"What are you talking about? Come on."

They walked back to the party and, although Esmé felt better, she decided that she would like a bit more fresh air before she went back inside. Her friend was cold so she went back to the party but Mike said that he didn't feel the weather and would like to walk with her for a while. They walked down to the train station where two years before I had told Josie that I loved her for the first time.

"You know my hands feel a bit cold," said Mike. She took his hand in hers and they walked back to the party. By the time they got there they were completely in love. The months before she went to Florida, they would walk down the promenade in Bexhill every night that Mike wasn't working and look into each other's eyes adoringly. Mum said Esmé had finally become a sickening teenager but she didn't mind, and she still managed to get straight As in her A-levels.

Those marks didn't stop her from being beside herself when the long distance relationship didn't work out between her and Mike. When it ended over the phone she paced up and down her room not knowing what to do. Still, she somehow managed to finish her year in Florida as an enthusiastic Minnie Mouse and came out with even more glowing references.

After her year in Florida she moved to Switzerland to start her PhD in Medicine at Basel University. She called Mum every night of her seven-year course and ended each call "I love you."

When Esmé finished her degree she became involved with the university's research facility where she met the Swiss academic, Dr. Pecon Karlsson, who was part of the department. Together they discovered a way to streamline chemotherapy so that its effectiveness went up by fifty percent. This helped to save cancer victims around the world and their work still affects countless people to this day. But the waves began to swell again. She wanted to go and help children in third-world countries and, despite protests from Dr. Karlsson, she went off to Soweto in 2023, kissing him goodbye in a rainy Samedan Airport. When she arrived in South Africa, she met another volunteer named Paul Manner. After six months of helping to build an orphanage, and despite every precaution, Esmé became pregnant with her daughter, Michelle. As soon as she found out, they both flew back to England and we were all present at the birth in Conquest Hospital in Hastings. Mum was crying and even Dad looked like he was shedding a few tears.

*　*　*

I watch Esmé now that she is old and grey, looking back on her long and happy life. She is looking down at her watch, still frozen in time since the early hours of the 20th December when she was walking back from Tesco. The time of her sudden death.

I always knew that life was unfair but I didn't know just how savage it could be. William Faulkner said that "time is dead as long as it is being clicked off by little wheels; only when the clock stops does time come to life." This doesn't make much sense to me. Does it make sense to you?

Which version of my sister's life I personally believe I am unable to say. All I know is that her watch stopping and her life ending at the age of eighteen cannot be right. It is ridiculous.

"To Allah we belong and to Him we shall return."
Sürah Al Baqarah 2:156

MICHÈLE BARZEY is a writer and theologian. She is interested in how the creative, theological and political interact with and inform each other, and the way the spoken word blurs the boundaries between poetry, prose and drama. More of her work can be found at http://afrobehnpoet.wordpress.com/.

One is One and All Alone
by Michèle Barzey

Even after all these years, I can still hear the music and the faint strains of the children's laughter as they vanished into Koppelberg Hill and out of our lives. 22nd July 1376. That was the day Hamelin changed, the day the rats ruined my life. Again.

My mother told me about the first time. I was two months old when the rats got me. If my screams hadn't eventually woken my drunken nursemaid it wouldn't have just been my foot I'd lost. Sometimes I think that that wouldn't be a bad thing. Anything was better than being the only child left in Hamelin Town.

No one had to tell me about the second time; I was there, in the midst of it. The rats were part of our lives; we had no choice but to learn to live with them. They were everywhere, in the houses, in the streets, in all the public buildings, ravaging the homes of rich and poor alike.

Over the years the rats got bigger, and bolder, and stronger. They didn't just skitter around in the dark and hide when people were around, they came right out into the light. We were the cleanest town in Brunswick. No one dared to drop litter. We tried everything, every kind of trap and poison, but nothing got rid of them. Whenever you killed one, ten took its place.

Then one day *he* came to town. No-one saw him arrive, but my sister Steffi and I, we were there when a tall thin man with long blonde hair, a dark face, and eyes that couldn't decide whether they were blue or green, strode out of the Town Hall with the Mayor and the council at his heels. There was a swirl of colours against the pristine white buildings of the square. He wore an old-fashioned frock coat, with one side red and the other yellow. His tunic and leggings were orange and his boots were red and on the yellow and red striped scarf knotted around his neck hung a dark, wooden flute.

But the strangest thing about him wasn't the way he dressed. It was the almost tangible silence that seemed to surround him. You need to understand: back then Hamelin was never quiet. The only thing that scared the rats away was noise and lots of it. We couldn't even eat in peace. There'd have to be someone singing or making noise at mealtimes otherwise the bolder ones would try and snatch food from our plates.

When he saw us staring at him open-mouthed, he winked and his smile said "Come dance, seize life by the throat and live it to the full!" He lifted the flute from where it rested on his chest, caressed it gently as if it was alive and needed assuring that it was all right to sing, then tossed his hair over his shoulder and began to play.

Over the years I've tried to explain what happened but it's still hard to find the words. You shouldn't have been able to hear the music over the din. When Steffi and I pushed through the crowds to get to the Town Hall we had had to shout to get ourselves heard. Yet as he played the sounds of the market became part of the melody until all you could hear was the music.

And as he played, he swayed. Shrieks and screams came from every quarter, we soon found out why. Rats. Rats pouring out of the houses. A living, flowing river of rats squeaking and squealing and pushing and shoving. Then the piper began to dance. He danced down the High Street and through the Town gates and when he reached the River Weser he waded in until the water was waist high. He carried on piping and the rats followed him. Wave after wave of them entered the river and were swept away. When he finally stopped playing there wasn't a single rat left on the riverbank.

The Mayor called for the Town Hall bell to be rung. When everyone had gathered in the square, he ordered that all the nests be dug out, all the holes blocked, and every street and building scoured from top to bottom, so that not a single rat would be left in Hamelin. As he was finishing his proclamation, there came a cheer from the outskirts of the crowd. A path opened up and the piper made his way to the Town Hall steps. The crowd fell silent and waited for him to speak. He bowed and waved, then turned to the Mayor and the Council and said, "Before you start the clearing up, can I have my thousand guilders please?"

The Council looked stunned, then rushed him into the Town Hall. Steffi and I sneaked in behind them.

The piper repeated his request. "A thousand Guilders, please."

The Mayor said, "You do realise we were joking don't you? Have fifty Guilders for your trouble."

"I've kept my side of the bargain," the piper said. "You keep yours."

The Council huddled together. Steffi and I looked at each other. For the first time we realized how much like rats they were. Some were stout and fat, others thin and wiry; what they all had in common was the greed in their eyes and the viciousness in their smiles. We half expected to see tails peeking out from beneath their robes.

They turned back to the piper. "You've solved our problem. The rats won't be coming back. Be grateful for your fifty and be on your way."

"I'm warning you," said the piper. "You don't want me to play a different tune."

"Play what you like," said the Mayor. "But not here."

"Very well," said the piper.

Once again he stood on the Town Hall steps, once again he tossed his hair over his shoulder, and once again he caressed his flute and raised it to his lips. And then he began to play and to sway. He played such beautiful music. I have never heard the like, before or since, except in my sleep. He promised to take us to a land where horses flew and dragons roamed, where the colours of the flowers made his clothes look drab, where I could throw away my crutches and run like a deer.

When he played for the rats, we could hardly stop our feet from tapping, but when he played for us, we had to dance.

Out of every house and schoolroom, out of every street and alley, laughing children came dancing to his call. In the excitement I lost sight of Steffi but at the time I didn't think it mattered. We danced through the streets - yes, even me on my crutches - and our parents stood and watched us go, tears streaming down their faces. But they never stopped us. It wasn't until afterwards that I found out that while the music played none of the adults could move. As we danced south towards the River Weser, our parents became more frantic. They thought we were going to go the way of the rats, but we knew our future lay elsewhere. The piper turned at the river and headed towards Koppelberg Hill. That's when I began to lose ground. I thought they'd slow down to climb the hill, that I'd have a chance to catch up, but the piper played a peculiar trill and a cavern opened up in front of them. I tried to move faster but I kept on stumbling, and falling further behind. When the cavern closed and the music died away I was left outside, on my own.

I cried then, I cried for my sister and I cried for the promises that would never come true. I was still crying when the townspeople arrived. My mother ordered the servants to carry me home and put me to bed. I slept for two days, and when I woke, it was still true.

After that, I was never allowed to go anywhere on my own. Not that I wanted to, not after the first time a childless father tried to snatch me from the street. When I did go out I could feel the townspeople's eyes boring into my back as I passed. Even worse were the ones who couldn't bear to look at me. The ones who disappeared inside as soon as they saw me coming, but were never quick enough to hide the pain in their faces.

Sometimes in the night, I hear the music, I see the future the piper weaved into his song, and I see Steffi and the others getting further and further away until all I can hear is the faint strains of their laughter in the distance. I run after them, but it's always just a dream and I wake up crying: "Don't leave me behind! Don't leave me alone!"

TED BONHAM is a remarkably intelligent, wonderfully handsome and disarmingly charming young writer with a truly wicked sense of humour and an incredibly sharp eye. He sometimes enjoys discussing himself in sickeningly positive terms in the third person.

Train Untrained or Derailed No. 15
by Ted Bonham

    Something somewhat
washed out/ one too many times through the machine perhaps/
    or else smoke-stained and yellowing
like an ancient manuscript from the nineteen nineties/
    [he catches sight of his own reflection in a
spittle-flecked mirror]//

        William Basinski has a series of recordings called
  The   Disintegration   Loops/

I have been playing them backwards//
    It has been discovered that neurogenesis
        continues in the subventricular zone
and the hippocampus of the adult mammalian brain//

        Yet my thoughts are thunk through cataract
        clouding/
I am my own plural audience to a cave wall shadow
    happening
[there is a world behind me/ making me nervous]
    and I have been reading faces I used to know
on strangers I pass in the street//

        "She is beautiful/" my internal
monologue [/a cognitive dissonance]
    "but" /I am afraid/ "we are disagreed//"

"Let it run/" my tutor says/ It is "a game we play//"
      And everything tastes like aniseed now/
a black liquorice parody of synaesthesia//

  My aim is to insufflate you into existence/
to keep myself awake long enough that I find something
   new there/
     /there is a glitch in the soft where
I find myself humming melodies I do not know//

        Discovery is an unhitching of the mind/
   "a catch of the thread"
/[an] unravelling to a singularity of focus/

   a serene single thought's attempt to be expressed//

ADAM BRETT worked for Thames Valley and Hampshire Constabularies for nearly a decade before taking voluntary redundancy to concentrate on his writing. *You're Going to be in Trouble* is taken from his memoir, *You're Going to be a Psycho*. Adam is also a novelist, and writes for radio and TV.

You're Going to be in Trouble
by Adam Brett

"One in four women in the UK will experience domestic violence in their lifetime... On average, two women a week are killed by a violent partner or ex-partner."
Source: Womensaid.org

123 Bow Hay Lane was a magnificent house. On the outskirts of Exeter, it stretched about half a mile in every direction and had maintained many of its period features.

A shaggy lawn and flowerbeds welcomed visitors to the mostly-painted front door, framed in loose red bricks. Beyond that, taking the creaking iron gate to the side of the house, the back yard ran long into the horizon, laid to great swathes of glorious mud and a coal bunker, which in turn was home to every type of spider and creepy-crawly one could ever hope to discover. There was even an outside toilet, negating the inconvenience of removing muddy shoes to go all the way into the house. Admittedly, some trips to that extremely cold outbuilding in the winter did end up lasting rather longer than expected, as occasionally, following matters that required more accurate, seated attention, an adult was needed to help prize numb legs from plastic.

One morning I was standing in the front garden, frowning at a bare patch of mud between bushes at the foot of our impressive bay window. It must have been two full hours since I had planted the seed, and still no apple tree. At that rate I considered it might well be two or even three days before I was presented with anything edible. Not that *I* would have eaten an apple, you understand.

The idea spawned from my good friend, Christopher Vowles,

or rather his older brother, Alan, who had warned us of what would happen if we ate any apple seeds. Despite this very real danger, Christopher's mother had insisted he was to take one of these sinister fruits to school every day, and there should be evidence of its consumption by way of a neatly trimmed core in his lunchbox come his return home. As such, I agreed to be his spotter, watching carefully after every bite, lest infant branches should begin to creep from his nostrils. That was until we realised that apples were something of a currency in the playground.

Bizarrely, girls actually liked them, and wholly indifferent to the horror that might befall them, would happily swap apples for infinitely superior Trios or Breakaways without even having to agree to be best friends, a contract which clearly would have provoked ridicule among our male counterparts. I thought then that if I had my own tree, there was room enough in my *Return of the Jedi* lunchbox for three, if not four apples, plus my own lunch, a wealth that might even secure lesser toys. At the same time, Christopher would simply ask for one of the cores back to place in his *Empire Strikes Back* lunchbox, and pass it off as his own.

The excitement was almost too much, but I was becoming sceptical of the supposed accelerated growth Alan had described. Certainly the small amount of bread and the sprinkling of sugar I had added did not seem to be encouraging anything to happen, and although I had now drenched the mud in water, I thought I might be just one bucket short.

I walked around to the outside tap to fill up again, when I was confronted with my sister, Leigh, bounding towards me in her white puffer suit.

"Mum needs us to find some tissue," she said cheerily, pulling her hood open enough to look over the full extent of the mess I had made in the garden.

She needs *us* to find tissue? I was quite certain she knew where to find it herself. Occasionally I would be called upon to help locate items in ground level cupboards, or a rogue dinosaur on the carpet, but it was altogether more usual that mum should tell me where to find things.

With the huff of a gardener interrupted, I dropped my bucket and kicked off my shoes at the door, making for the stairs.

Unusually, once inside, there was no sound, and as I had almost reached the first floor I was not entirely sure anyone else was in. My sister followed close behind, holding her hood open with two miniature digits in a letterbox of sorts across her face. Was this a game? Was dad going to jump out at us? Was Leigh in on this? It was hard to make out whether or not she was smiling in that ridiculous coat, but then, Leigh thought everything was funny, even more so than I.

I might have started an interrogation if it wasn't for a sudden jump as our parents' door flung open. My dad swept out and strode quickly past us, down the stairs. He didn't say a word, looking through us as though we weren't there. A few moments later and the front door was heard to open and shut. He was gone.

Leigh and I looked at each other in confusion, and then back at the door from where he had emerged, now slightly ajar.

I slowly paced the landing towards the door, listening carefully for any sign of life, but any sound there might have been was shouted down by an angry engine and screaming tyres as our car left the road.

Pushing the door open, I peeked around to see mum lying on the bed, fully clothed. She was facing away from me and clutching a crumpled tissue about her waist. She seemed to breathe heavily and shake somewhat, perhaps suffering with the effects of a cold.

At that point Leigh brushed into the room behind me, clutching an entire bouquet of toilet paper.

"Got it, mum," she said, pleased with her discovery and holding her arms outstretched in front of her.

Mum sat up and swung her legs around to perch on her side of the bed, her head bowed under a mop of long blonde curls. But she would not turn to face us, something that for reasons unknown made me feel extremely uneasy. Hers was the face I always wanted to see the most. It brought calm and reassurance with a simple flash of those bright blue eyes, smiled when I was silly, and chased nightmares away when it appeared in my darkened room at night. But as we rounded that bed, it was not the same face.

A flawless sheen of pale skin eventually gave way to a tortoiseshell of black, yellow and purple. Her left ear had cried a single tear of red, matting some hair tight to her neck, while those bright eyes had surrendered to a maze of thin, stinging ivy. Looking closer she seemed to lean uncomfortably to that one side, as she took the tissue from my sister and held it to the side of her head.

"I'm okay," she said, "Don't worry."

I don't remember asking anything, only that I stood there for a while just looking. It could have been days, if not weeks before I fully understood what had really happened, if not why. But one thing I did know is that when *I* fell, I bled, and that in my bravado when I said that it didn't hurt, I knew full well that it did.

That morning is where it started for me, and in the years that followed my sister and I were to play nurse for our mother more times than any young mind should be asked to recall. Despite our repeated attempts to appease this man - to make him happy, to live up to his expectations and maintain the comical pretence of a family united - we lived in the constant fear that one minor detail missed could wake the beast.

Home was the very last place I wanted to be, and I did everything I could to keep myself from the confines of those walls. I would stay out in the evenings for as long as possible, running or cycling as far away as I was allowed to be seen with friends, or if I was on my own, simply hiding away in alleyways or up trees.

Sometimes I would stray onto another estate, watching people do nothing in particular and inventing stories of who they were in my mind. The man putting out the bins had killed his children and was disposing of them. The lady parking her car opposite was the police and she was watching him. The old couple, who often caught me idly staring into windows, they were brother and sister who had escaped their evil family, hidden behind a landfill of pot plants and forever disguised in regulation geriatric beige.

I was careful to time excursions according to the general mood in the house. When I had returned home from school and there was calm, I knew that I could make for the far reaches of my allotted territory and pretty much wait to be called back in. Sometimes there would be a miniature messenger in the form of a friend's younger sister advising that tea was ready. In any case, this allowed a few more precious minutes as I developed a sudden lethargy, or perhaps even a curious knee injury that slowed my return. As long as I remembered to be polite and grateful when I was finally sat at the table and presented with my dinner, I might get away with it. But there were limits.

If I had underestimated the length of a bike journey, or neglected to watch the clock in a friend's house, pushing the needle past the five-minutes-late barrier and into the red, then I had no choice but to steel myself for what was to follow. I had tried any number of excuses - I'm sure I even suggested I was being held hostage once - it wouldn't matter. Five minutes was far too late, and children who are far too late are smacked.

My father's mood would only grow darker with the winter, a season that snatched whole hours of my freedom each night, forcing us all to share more time together and suffer the inevitable consequences this brought about.

There were only two consolations during this period. The first was waiting for my sister to fall asleep for around an hour and then waking her up, pretending that seven in the evening was in fact seven in the morning, and she should go downstairs to put her school uniform on. Even dad thought that was funny. I would watch from the top of the stairs as the bleary little girl murmured nonsense, half asleep, trying to put her skirt on her head.

The second was the promise of Christmas, and two if not three days of genuine laughter and happiness. It was still a delicate balance, but my mother and I learned to work as a team, keeping tabs on how much dad had drunk at any given point, bringing up subjects and suggestions accordingly during the day.

My father could certainly never blame drink for his twenty-four-hour disposition – he very rarely drank at all as I recall, and we never went to a single pub – but when he did decide upon a few cans, we knew that we had to maintain order until at least the third hiss of a ring pull before we could all relax. Any earlier and the alcohol could swing his mood inexplicably in the other direction. The familiar stare would precede a deliberately provocative question, completely at random, such as asking mum why it took so long to come back from the shops, or worse, the venomous topic of coin might have cause to barge our discourse. No answer would do, however friendly or abrupt, let alone true. That would be the end of another night.

Perhaps it was that my timing was out during our last Christmas together. It had started well enough. Christmas Eve was a cosy affair with smiles and chocolates. Dad was even teasing us about what Father Christmas may have in store the following morning, building excitement to the point that I actually asked to go to bed, hoping the morning might come quicker; a comment that at any other time of the year would have demanded the immediate introduction of a thermometer.

When morning did come I remember an incredible glow. Our stockings were full to bursting at the foot of our beds, and this was just the appetiser. Running downstairs in our pyjamas, the pile of presents had quadrupled in size under the tree, more than I ever could have realistically tried to open at the corner for a sneak peek.

The bounty belied our precarious financial position. It was if our parents had decided that no matter what, we will enjoy this day; we will be a family; we will forget what has gone before. Our lives start now. In reality, and however much we might have wanted to, I don't think any of us believed that.

As Christmas dinner piped hot steam into the dining room, things were going too well. We were all seated at the table, crackers pulled, paper hats on, surrounding the colourful entrails of a party popper hanging from the lampshade. My baby brother, James, wriggled in his high chair, straining to grab at anything close enough. Leigh was finishing some colouring in her new book featuring all the happily-ever-after Disney princesses, and I was flying my *He-Man* figure, Buzz-off, around my chair.

Mum entered with the first plates of food, overflowing with moist, clean slices of turkey, crisp potatoes and vegetables. It must have been half my body weight in pure indulgence, and there was certainly more than I could ever have finished. Unfortunately for us that day, we would not be allowed a choice.

I think I must have seen dinner as a distraction from playing with my new toys. I remember that I was literally forcing turkey into my mouth, trying to wash it down my throat with squash when chewing failed.

Dad was watching me, the only reason why I continued to eat, despite the sensation of food congealing in my throat, poised to reappear at any point. In the end I simply had to concede defeat and put down my knife and fork.

Mum did her best to ignore this, and with fleet of thought tried to distract dad with a question about one of the guide dogs he had been training. His glare had not moved from my plate, however, a situation compounded when Leigh looked over to see I had finished and followed suit.

"Finish your dinner," he said, clutching his knife tightly in one hand, his fork stuck through a piece of meat in the other.

"I can't," I said, meekly.

"Finish your dinner," he repeated, his posture still fixed.

"I can't. I'm full."

"Eat it. *Now*"

"I can't" I protested, trying desperately to hold back the tears I knew he hated so much.

He jumped from his seat, ripping the hat from his head and throwing his cutlery onto the ceramic, which squealed in protest. With one hand he slapped a crystal glass up against the wall, narrowly missing my mother's head. With the other he launched his plate across the room, splashing a stain up the wall as the jagged shrapnel stabbed our Christmas tree. He continued round the table, destroying everything within range.

"Gary, stop!" pleaded my mother, as James' beaker was swiped from his tiny hands, provoking an ear-splitting scream.

My sister was pushed from her chair as the last obstacle between us and I was torn from my seat to be shaken at the shoulders. I forget what he said to me. I was rigid with fear in his grasp, tightening my body for the strikes to follow before I was dumped on the carpet, stuck with glass that was still falling in drops from the walls. He slapped my sister across the face: "Stop crying."

Shakin' Stevens was oblivious, still happily wishing us a merry Christmas on TV as dad did what he always did following an episode and left the room, footsteps crunching and tearing at the floor. My mother picked James from his high-chair to cradle him in her arms, wiping tears away with her forearm and glass from his beaker as she gently tried to bob him back to calm.

I never found out where he went each time this happened; whether it was simply somewhere quiet to stew in the car, or to see someone in particular. Who would you talk to? Mum would come to suggest that he might have found solace in the arms of another woman, perhaps making up a story of his suffering among the gormless creatures he was forced to co-habit with, but I could never see how he could attempt a rational conversation with anyone in the aftermath of each incident.

In any case there would be no apology, there never was. There would only be a silence, gradually eroded with simple, short, necessary questions, until we were safe enough to act as though nothing had happened again.

This time around, however, my mother had made concrete a decision. She had already begun digging our escape, and determined that we should not suffer another cycle on this hideous merry-go-round, we would run.

It can only have been a few weeks on from that day that I left school one afternoon to find her standing at the gates with Leigh, James in his pram and two suitcases.

"We're going on holiday," she said.

Technically, I'm still on that holiday, one that has seen us journey through stigma and stepfamilies and back out again. In twenty years, six schools and two police forces, I would come to re-evaluate what I saw as the 'normal' family, as at first a victim, then an onlooker, and finally as an advisor with the police.

RICHARD BURKE has recently turned his hand to short story writing after many years as a lyricist and songwriter. He has just had a story published in University of Chester's *Flash* magazine of international story writing.

The Mermaid Tank
by Richard Burke

In the town of Rathwire, there is a small petting zoo. The enclosures of farmyard animals, mute and starved, line the path which leads to a small building from the Victorian era.

Once through the heavy oak door and into the clammy, dark room, the visitor is faced with a large, empty glass tank.

A polite notice, faded by sunlight, explains that the Mermaid is currently absent due to a sudden illness. There are newspaper clippings on the far wall which date back to the early 1900s. They show pictures of proud gentlemen surrounding a young girl whose lower half is obscured by a sign announcing her unveiling. The articles say that she travelled from afar and speaks little English. Her eyes in the photograph appear as small balls of cold, dark granite and her mouth is a thin, black line.

There are small, smudged fingerprints all around the outside of the tank where the sticky hands of children once vyed for space. The olive green algae inside the glass is pocked with tiny marks as if fish scales have been dragged through it. Along the floor of the tank is a dark crimson patch which appears to have once been a large puddle. This has been smeared onto the glass long ago and left to dry.

The sun descends in the early evening. Darkness envelopes the musty room as the small animals in the petting zoo begin to stir.

MIKE B. CAHILL is an English and Creative Writing graduate of the School of English at Birmingham City University. His writing credits include *Van der Graff Man* and a short story published in the *In the Red* anthology. He regularly reviews in the Brumbeat magazine and produces copy, web content and press releases for a well known music industry brand.

Mike is working on his first novel, the tale of a cross-dressing widow and an awkward teenage boy set in an otherworldly 1950s rural England.

New York 1985
by Michael B. Cahill

"And then it dawned on me; he was actually going to pull the trigger"

Eddie Woods

Lately I've been dreaming about Mexico, about Joan, Bill and Lewis. I wake wracked by the pointlessness of it, the stupidity, and I'm left with a deep sense of waste. As I get closer to the end the dreams are becoming more frequent, more vivid. In the dreams Joan looks fine and well, the way she looked before tequila and salt made her strange, before the bullet in her temple.

Joan was kind of plain looking, her straight hair bedraggled, she wore faded flower-print dresses and always seemed to be barefoot. She always seemed a little high too, whether it was drink or something else I don't know. Joan had used Benzedrine inhalers for years, sometimes ten a day, according to Lewis. They were difficult to get in Mexico so she weaned herself off them and on to Tequila: for breakfast, for lunch, for dinner. She drank one and a half, maybe two, bottles a day - Billy Jnr. and Julie were left to run wild.

That day, in Healy's apartment, where Lewis and me were staying, we were all sober... maybe not Bill, I never could tell with Bill. Joan and Bill came by late in the afternoon and she had brought a drink from down stairs - cheap Mexican gin mixed with Limonada, which is like 7Up, in a high-ball glass; Healy wouldn't let Joan put Tequila on tab.

Joan and Bill were a strange pair. She was highly intelligent; every bit Bill's equal - if not his superior. They would argue and debate, sometimes long into the night, she would match him wit for wit. They didn't seem to be in love, not in the accepted sense of the word. I never saw Bill show affection for Joan (apart from him calling her Joanie); she was interesting to him, in some way, that's all. They had had a physical side, a sexual side; Joan once told me that Bill was a skilled lover, the best she'd ever had, and with him being a fruit. Bill made no secret of his liking for boys. I remember him remarking about sex with women, I can hear that tedious drawl: *women are like tortillas, they keep you alive, nourish you, but what you really want is steak*. Bill had been living on tortillas for a week, on account of being flat broke.

Healy's apartment was above the Bounty Bar and Grill, a rundown place on the corner of Monterrey and Chihuahua. It was still hot that September in Mexico City. The windows were open but there was no street noise. Everything was so still, just the whir of the ceiling fan. Then there was this whistle, from a knife sharpener as he rode past on his route. It cut right through. I didn't recognise the tune, but it has somehow stuck with me.

Healy was downstairs working. Bill wanted to use Healy's place to sell one of his hand guns, a .38 auto, and didn't want the buyer to know where he lived. Bill also wanted witnesses, in case the deal went bad. There was something sinister about Bill; something I could never quite get. I always felt he was a bad influence on Lewis, all that talk of guns and dope. Bill had been running around after Lewis for quite some time, they'd just come back from a trip together, Ecuador or somewhere. I'd known Lewis for a couple of years and had never seen him go with another man. But Bill had this power, this strange influence, over Lewis. I never understood that.

Joan must have been aware of Lewis and Bill's situation. In fact, she and Lewis had been *real* good friends too. She was older than him, twenty eight; he was only twenty one. Lewis once remarked to me that he found Joan attractive in a *low-key sort of way*. Joan would have known this right from the outset; she had some weird telepathic ability. They played these games, Joan and Bill, these mindreading games. Sometimes it was eerie, the way she seemed to know what was going on inside other people's heads.

After I dream about Joan Vollmer I can never get back to sleep. I usually fix myself a drink and look out at the city; its electric miasma blinding the stars. I can't remember the last time I saw stars. The city's in constant motion, turning, its wheels grinding, round and round. A sodium haze bleeds through the night, infecting my perception; I can feel corporeal terror oozing through the walls; the machinery of the night will keep on turning with or without me... with or without Joan. When you know it's over all fear dissolves and you're left with a kind of calm, more than that, relief, and you simply accept what's coming, step off the machine, out of the fray.

When Bill and Joan arrived at Healy's - I'd not seen her for a while - she was walking with a cane; she'd had polio as a child and it had come back. The booze had bloated her features and her hair was thinning, she had sores too and some of her upper teeth were missing; she looked terrible, but it didn't register at the time. There was a kind of awful smell hanging in the air too, greasy and acrid, meaty and sour.

We sat, the four of us, together around a coffee table - Bill next to me, Joan opposite and Lewis in an armchair. Bill was talking about going back to Central America, how he'd live off the land, hunt wild boar. Joan, as she often would, began to mock him, in front of everyone. She laughed and said that if she and Julie and Billy Jnr. had to rely on Bill to hunt for food then they'd starve. There was a silence, a charged silence, then Bill took the .38 from a carry-all bag and said to Joan: *let's do the William Tell routine, Joanie, and show the boys what a fine shot old Bill is.*

I remember looking at Lewis who was looking at Bill and thinking how crazy it sounded. What the hell kind of routine was the *William Tell*? Anyway, Joan emptied her glass, turned side on, and sat up straight. She placed the highball carefully on her head. What she said next - which I thought nothing of at the time - haunts me. The look in her eyes, they seemed to have no depth at all. They looked artificial. And that half smile on her raw face... it still sends me cold. She stared right at me and said: *Hey, Eddie, I'd better close my eyes. You know I can't stand the sight of blood.*

I saw Bill raise his arm and take aim. I was within reach of him and I did nothing. I saw Bill lick his lizard lips, narrow his damaged-marble eyes and steady his breath. I did nothing. I saw Bill squeezing the trigger. I still did nothing. I saw Bill shoot Joan in the head. But Bill didn't kill her; Joan Vollmer Burroughs was already dead.

I fix myself another drink and shuffle back to the window. I look down at the street, at the hustlers and the hookers and the cops and the crazies. Could I have stopped Bill? Should I have stopped him?

It was as though Joan knew Bill would miss the glass. Like I said, she had telepathic abilities that I could never explain. It was as if she'd given up: on Bill, on Julie and Billy Jnr., on herself; the way a wounded animal, resigned to its fate, separates from the herd and lays down in peace. Did she read Bill's unconscious mind? I don't believe that Bill purposely killed Joan, I mean, it would've been a pretty elaborate double bluff, to do it in front of witnesses. But maybe, on some deep level, Bill wanted her out of the way. I don't know; maybe Lewis had got in between Bill and Joan. Maybe Bill was jealous. After all, he was crazy for Lewis.

After the shot Joan slumped in the chair and the glass fell to the floor. It didn't smash but rolled round and round on the lino. We thought, at first, that Joan was just kidding, but when we saw blood... I'll never forget the sound that Bill made, a kind of low howl, and he went to Joan and held her in his arms repeating her name over and over. Healy came upstairs to see what was going on. He called for the Cruz Roja and they came, and that was that.

The sun's coming up, casting long shadows west. As I stand

here looking out New York is born again, bathed in new light from an ancient sun; Selene gives way Helios. I see ghosts everywhere, spectres and angels, phantoms and fiends on the - how did Ginsberg put it? - *negro streets... looking for an angry fix.* I slump back into my armchair. My room is dead still, silent and musty, like an old oil painting. I let my eyes close and I drift; drift on the sea of salty slumber hoping to catch a glimpse, in the depths, of Joan, barefoot, faded flowers, her long bedraggled hair floating, ebbing and flowing, like strange seaweed.

TOM CLEMENTS' natural character is the entertainer who loves to make jokes in social situations. However, he enjoys challenging himself as a writer and tries to use his writing as a way to explore human emotions and dramas, even if it goes against his usual comedic tendencies.

Sit Down and Talk
by Tom Clements

Sit down and talk to me for a little while
and tell me about your life growing up,
growing old, but never as old as me.
Were they the best times of your life?
I mean, it can't have been *all* bad.
I know you had to make do without certain things
like good vision,
And a dad.

So I should weep? Fall to my knees?
I should beg for your forgiveness

But I won't, why should I?
You were kept a dirty little secret
even from me, was I not to be trusted? Or
were you not worth loving?
I loved your mother

For a night, of, less than passion…
Fun! Yes it was definitely fun.
We went our separate ways and you were born
A bastard.
I don't even know when you were born
though it was probably April 1st.
We fucked in the Summer, and now I'm the fool,
the father that won't acknowledge his son
as his own sun sets.

Yet I ask you about your life,
how was your life growing up, growing old?
You'll never be as old as me,
Yet I am told I've never grown wise.

After the sun sets the night will follow,
and the morning comes again
but it's too late for me,
I will never be a better man

I never want to be that man.

PAUL COSTELLO'S comedy writing is widely used by local am-dram and musical theatre, and he wrote the lyrics for *48-hour Musical* performed at the Mac, Birmingham in 2011. His new book *Utterly Undiscovered* is a Fawlty-inspired memoir of his Shropshire B&B. He works for Herefordshire Libraries, travels a lot and follows Brighton and Hove Albion.

Lardy Lee's Revenge
by Paul Costello

"Accident – Severe Delays," said the overhead warning signs.

You'd never know it was the rush hour. No rushing here - stuck for an hour, steaming up on a Lancashire motorway. Some relieve their boredom pacing the damp tarmac, others clamber the bank for different relief, thinking they're less conspicuous ten yards up the slope. The British in crisis: 'We'll all pull together' - or 'piss' in today's case. The French do it all the time.

I'd rather hunker down with Radio 4: Jamie Oliver and Hugh Dick-Whittington putting the world to rights. Even Eddie Mair can't get a word in. Does whiney Oliver really think a boy feels good finding half a papaya and a wedge of lime with his sandwiches, and his pals watching? An apple was sissy enough, I remember - and always got thrown to the goat across the playing field fence.

No doubt we'll reminisce about school dinners over the weekend; good fodder for reunions. Soggy vegetables and slices of grey meat swimming in thin gravy; lumpy custard made with water; and stodgy puddings. All under the watchful stare of Dead-Eye Doris...

* * *

Dead-Eye Doris only had one proper eye, which was china blue. The left one was made of glass. In the sixties artificial eyes were pretty basic. Whilst celebrities like Sammy Davis Junior could afford one that looked almost real, Dead-Eye's National Health variety, bluey-grey with veins, was a poor match and bulged in its socket.

Her eyes were also unusually far apart, which meant if she turned her head slightly to the right the proper eye disappeared from view and the glass one sat centrally in her high forehead like a Cyclops. Using our Geometry protractors as a guide (and not to draw sun or half-moon shapes and colour them in with crayon as they did down the secondary modern - or so we were told) we guessed that the required turn to achieve this look was about twenty degrees. And since this meant her mouth also turned to one side, she had to speak from the corner of pouted lips, adding to the general air of deformity. All in all she'd have made a better freak in a Victorian circus than a Head Cook in a Grammar School.

While the face was her most frightening attribute, Dead-Eye was a daunting figure in every respect. Though not tall, she was solidly built with muscular arms and no discernible waist. She'd stand at the hatches, chunky legs astride like a rugby player at the bar, a few inches of woollen socks over crinkled stockings showing below the discoloured white coat.

Nobody *ever* crossed Dead-Eye Doris. Under her barked instructions, the half dozen timid dinner ladies scurried between giant ovens, heads bowed so as not to catch her eye, and table monitors too approached with great trepidation. Commanding her territory like a Sherman tank in the desert, Dead-Eye would lean forward to line up the target, her false eye piercing into a boy's face, especially intimidating on a monitor's first ever visit to the hatches.

"What do you think you're doing, boy?" I'd heard her say to twelve year old Le Clerc on his initial encounter. Confused by the question, since it was obvious he'd come to collect the food, and not knowing whether to address the eye or the mouth round the corner, the dumbfounded novice was psychologically scarred for the rest of his school life.

On another occasion Le Clerc and I had fought at the hatches over second helpings of custard, tugging at an aluminium jug until the handle came off in Le Clerc's hand and the custard slopped into my blazer pocket. Dead-Eye, who'd had a ringside seat, made us replace the jug there and then; actually go out and buy another one. At least I'd won the custard, though being half French it was unlikely Le Clerc would ever win much anyway. After the fifth form he emigrated to Canada and was last seen dressed as The Marquis of Montcalm in a re-enactment of the Battle of Quebec - which the French still lost.

We never knew if Doris was her real name. But it went well with 'Dead-Eye' and showed that Grammar School boys were clever at weaving words, a skill that would have been spotted in the eleven-plus when we'd cut free from the ne'er-do-wells by answering more questions correctly. And to think - we might have landed up down the secondary modern, forced to recite the alphabet daily and cut out fuzzy-felt shapes before taking up a career in cleaning public toilets. Or so we were told. Instead, by getting four hundred and fifty out of seven hundred in the exam we were destined for careers as politicians or nuclear physicists. Four hundred and forty nine, and the toilets it would have been. Or so we were told.

I remember the first Friday after Lewniham started at the school. Fridays meant one thing – fish. Outside the canteen we'd queue in lines of ten, each row allotted to a table inside. As with most school matters these were arranged alphabetically – where you sat in class, where you stood in the school photo, the line-up in compulsory Cadet Corps – all decided by the first letter of your surname, a kind of military hangover. In the queue next to us, L to P, we heard Lewniham's thoughts on the subject.

"Fuckin' fish, fuck 'em," he called out in an agitated manner. "Fuck it. Fuckin' fish."

"Why does he talk like that?" I said to Cornichon in front of me.

Nicknamed Gherkin, Cornichon scoured the NME with me every Friday morning at the back of the class, noting the climbers and fallers in the Top 40 Charts. We'd always intended forming a band to follow in the footsteps of the Shadows or Billy Fury. One day after school we visited the instrument shop by

Brighton Clock Tower where as lead guitarist I bought a shiny Spanish guitar, and Cornichon a small cymbal for his drum kit. We weren't quite sure what to do with them, but it was a start. Well, it was a finish actually – we never did buy anything else.

"Dunno," he said. "Bit rough, isn't he?"

"Oi, Butlin – you camp or something?" Lewniham yelled across to Butlin further down our queue. "You a fuckin' queer?" Apparently Lewniham had stayed at a Butlins holiday resort that summer and must have thought this was funny. Butlin just ignored him.

"He was the same in football on Wednesday," said Darke behind me. "Kept kicking my ankles and saying 'yer tit, yer tit' like a parrot."

Darke and I got on well. The 'e' was silent but we changed it to a 'y' on account of his jet black hair and how easily he tanned. Half an hour fishing on Brighton beach in winter sunshine and he'd look darker than the rest of us would after three months of summer sun.

We all had nicknames but Gherkin and Darky got off lightly compared with another mate Cathole who, despite his protestations that it was pronounced like "catholic", was known by the two words that made up his surname.

Personally, I was grateful for the nickname Capsello, after a well-known Italian footballer, acknowledging my skills with a tennis ball – one-touch control before slamming a goal between the bike shed uprights.

Lewniham had come to the school unexpectedly. He was a marginal eleven-plusser, a four-hundred-and-forty-niner, who on a better day might have remembered what two and two came to and scored the extra points needed to avoid the Palace Pier toilets. Or so we were told.

He said that down the secondary modern he'd shown the other boys how to use a protractor properly, to the chagrin of the teachers whom it showed up in a poor light, and had begun to string words together alliteratively (he even knew the meaning of that word) with the idea of becoming a writer when he left school. He showed us a piece he'd written for his father to give to the Headmaster, Mr Bloggins, as evidence that an injustice had been done:

> "I really, really would rather read and write up the Grammar School, where I've heard that dinners are dished out daily by Dead-Eye Doris."

Once he'd read this, Mr Bloggins agreed that Lewniham had been wrongly sent to the secondary modern and deserved the chance of a career in corporate management or space travel. With places tight this wasn't easy and the matter was not handled well. Another marginal called Wayster was hauled out of Geography by a prefect and apparently despatched into the same taxi that minutes earlier had dropped off Lewniham and his dad for an elaborate welcome in Mr Bloggins' study.

Little did Mr Bloggins realise what he'd let himself in for. You can keep the boy out of the toilets, but you can't take the toilet out of the boy. Most of us hadn't been brought up with swearing. We knew what "swear words" sounded like, but didn't know what they meant or what to do with them. If we tried, it would come out wrong, like:

"I don't fancy PE today, bloody it."

And when we tried looking them up in the school dictionary the pages were usually defaced or missing. Lewniham's language therefore remained something of a mystery, but he used a lot of swear words a lot of the time.

"Fuckin' Crabbe's a fuckin' twat, fuck 'im," he'd say about the History master. We'd just mutter and nod.

"I ain't bloody going in goal," he'd say when the House football team was put on the board. "Fuck 'em, they can fuckin' find some other fucker." We'd smile to show we were right there with him.

"He's okay most of the time," I told my mother. "He looks

normal and smiles quite a bit, but it's the swearing. He does it all the time. That's not normal, is it?"

"Hm, but 'Lewniham', dear. I do wonder with a name like that."

She seemed shocked when I repeated his words and thought it might be a result of his time at the secondary modern where they all talked like that. Or so she'd been told. Then she asked:

"Do you know if he's got the Tourettes?"

"I don't think so," I said, not having heard of them. "I don't think he follows the charts. More into jazz, I think."

My mother, who'd been a nurse, went on to explain that Lewniham's behaviour might be linked to a mental condition.

"Sometimes they keep repeating words that don't make sense," she said. "It's not his fault. You shouldn't worry about it too much."

I asked her what some of the words meant. She explained that "bastard" meant a boy who didn't have a proper father, so it wasn't very kind calling people that.

"And what does 'cunt' mean?" I asked. "He says that a lot."

"It'll be the Tourettes," she said, unable to explain. None of the other boys' mothers knew either, but we guessed it was something nasty.

"Well it's not all bad," I said. "At least his swearing is good alliteration. That would have been wasted down the secondary modern. Or so he says."

At first Lewniham would yell to no-one in particular, as if he was angry with all of us.

"Shit shit shit!" we'd hear echoing round the boys' toilets, which even there seemed a bit over the top. "Shit shit shit shit!" - like a steam engine labouring up a steep gradient.

But not long after he arrived he began targeting Lee. It started in small ways, barging into him in the corridor or just staring. And then the swearing took hold.

"You're a fat bastard, Lee!" he'd say in class, loud enough

for most of *us* to hear but not the teacher. "Oi! Lardy Lee! You fuckin' eat too much, you fat cunt!"

Admittedly, Lee was pretty large. His tiny head and giant torso were of snowman proportions and his bum jiggled as he walked. It didn't help that he wore thick pebble glasses and often began sentences with "I say you fellows", like Billy Bunter on the TV. I felt sad thinking he didn't have a proper dad.

On any ordinary day in the canteen, table monitors would have been terrified going up to the serving hatches. But one extraordinary Friday there was a rush to get there. It was the day Dead-Eye Doris lost her glass eye. Mr Pettiman, a junior English teacher whose turn it was to supervise the canteen, had told the queues to be sympathetic towards her, but that was the last thing likely to happen. Some boys saw it as a great opportunity to get their own back on Dead-Eye for being so nasty. Quite how they intended to do so wasn't clear since most of them wouldn't dare say anything, but safely outside in the queue there was much sniggering and an air of anticipation.

We heard what had happened from one of the dinner ladies, Minnie, who'd bumped into Lee's mother in Woolworths. Dead-Eye's glass eye had popped out during a violent coughing fit and rolled away like a marble, and her good one had watered so much from coughing that she didn't see where the marble had gone. An intensive search began – in cupboards and drawers, under cookers and down drains - but to no avail.

Dead-Eye would have felt horribly exposed. She'd have known it was the singular stare that gave her control, and that an empty socket or eye patch would weaken her hold. But proving that she wasn't just a cranky old tank and that there was a brain inside that cyclopic head, she'd devised a great way to get through the dinner hour.

As well as deliveries from large catering companies, the Head Cook could buy supplies from local sources if she thought the food fresher or better value. So, even though any extra nutritional value was lost baking it in an overheated oven to a dry, rubbery texture, so that it came out the same regardless of what it was or where it had come from, Dead-Eye bought fresh fish every week from a Brighton merchant.

On that particular Friday she'd taken a consignment of whole haddock. The fish was prepared on site; heads, tails and fins cut away roughly with a cleaver and the carcass chopped into cutlets, bone in, skin on – much as a butcher would chop a rack of lamb, but with less finesse. The fish was then ready for baking to death.

Dead-Eye had noticed several heads poking up in the large stock pot where off-cuts were waiting to be boiled for a sauce. She'd tossed the contents around until the head of what might have been a twelve pound haddock came to the surface, and with a sharp kitchen knife she'd carefully cut round the sinewy flesh holding in its left peeper. The fresh and staring haddock eye filled most of her socket, and the fishy mucus seemed to hold it steady. "It'll do," thought Dead-Eye, but to the dinner ladies it looked creepy and unnatural.

I sensed that Lewniham was pleased about the missing eye. Convinced he'd built a bond with Dead-Eye - if this was the case he'd be the only boy ever to have done so – he was probably wondering how, as table monitor, he could use it to his advantage. Perhaps if he showed extra sympathy or even found the missing eyeball he'd get larger portions or be allowed up first for second helpings. And with Lee on his table this would be handy, since food went missing from other boys' plates as soon as they looked away. But if Lewniham *was* thinking these things it didn't show, for he was too busy goading Lee.

"You're a prick, Lee," he said, shoving him into the queue. "Piss off, you prickhead."

Lee wasn't afraid of Lewniham, and guessed the rest of the queue would be on his side.

"Dead-Eye's lost her dead eye, Dead-Eye's lost her dead eye," he chanted, trying to get the others singing like at a football match. He'd seen Lewniham trying to get in Dead-Eye's good books and knew the chanting would rankle him. "I say you fellows, Dead-Eye's lost her dead eye…"

Lewniham turned on him harder and a scuffle ensued. Normal activity in the queues died away as the fight took hold. Boys in F to K put aside their Chinese puzzles and I quickly finished a coin transaction in A to E, pocketing a couple of shiny, late-Victorian pennies chipped around the edge, probably by a tram.

"Fuck, fuck, fuck, you fat fucker," said Lewniham, his voice hammering like a road drill.

"I say old fellow, you don't frighten me," said Lee.

They fell to the ground and rolled about on the dusty concrete until two dinner prefects separated them; just as well, because with Lee on top it could have got nasty. Lewniham was given a Saturday detention, but didn't seem to care, and Lee was let off.

"Is dinner ready soon?" Lee asked them. As we later found out, this wasn't just because he was hungry but because he had a cunning plan.

"Stand for grace," said Mr Pettiman, setting off a cacophony of clattering benches as the backs of boys' knees insidiously flicked the five-seaters to the ground.

After, "For what we are about to receive, may the Lord make us truly thankful," or as we would have it, "For what we are about to leave, may the pigs be truly grateful," he added an extra prayer, proving his own alliterative skills:

"And let us pray that the Head Cook's missing marble may be found, and that our brave boys will help her wholeheartedly at the hatches."

"Ah-oong," we muttered, the closest we ever got to "amen", before sitting down to await instructions, At the end of my bench Cornichon's fingers banged out the drum roll from Tommy Roe's *Sheila* on the scrubbed pine table, although without the added 'sher-shoong' bass line we'd hardly have recognised it. Waiting to be called to the hatches was taking longer than usual, giving time on L to P for Lewniham to resume his attack. At a prearranged signal the four other boys on Lee's bench stood up, making it flip like a see-saw. Lee, who'd been forced to sit at one end, toppled to the floor and lay there like a beached whale.

"Get up you fat, lardy bastard," said Lewniham, falsely using his authority as table monitor.

Lee levered himself up, unruffled. We realised afterwards he must have felt impervious to this aggravation, knowing that he was about to get his own back.

As usual the boy in charge of the staff table was called up first. This week it was Darke from ours. The staff table was on a raised platform at one end of the canteen, less for them to spot miscreant behaviour, which was left to the hapless junior teacher on duty, than to appear important. They also had superior food, better presented. Their fish would be a thick, skinned fillet of whatever the boys were having, fried in a light batter and garnished with a curl of parsley and lemon wedge. The vegetables, unlike ours still recognisable, were served in china dishes, with a matching jug for thick parsley and lemon sauce.

This is what Darke now went up to fetch. All eyes were on the hatches. Dead-Eye was too far away for us to see clearly, but we sensed she'd lost her usual fire. We saw Darke peering none too subtly at her face and a frightened look crossing his own. Having delivered the tasty-looking food to the raised table, he scurried back to ours.

"It's alive," he said.

"What is?" we asked, urgently.

"The eye," he said, "it's green and moves around."

"Does it still stare?" I asked.

"No, it's got a life of its own. It wanders everywhere. I couldn't look after a while."

At that point table monitors were called up and a mad rush ensued. Boys who normally took detours round the room to delay meeting Dead-Eye made a beeline for the hatches. As A to E monitor I was first in line to see what she'd done.

Dead-Eye's head was at its usual angle, dead eye front – only it wasn't dead. Where there'd once been a rigid, grey-blue eye, there was now a flexible green object with a large black centre, sliding in slime with no clear sense of direction. During my minute at the hatches it glided round the socket from the centre to the left boundary, rebounding slowly to the right, then slipping downwards to expose a gaping hole before re-centring itself. As it moved, the shape changed like jelly, round in the centre and elliptical at each extreme. It was like a pinball machine in slow motion – utterly hypnotic.

"Here's your fish. I hope you like it," said Dead-Eye in a surprisingly polite way. With other monitors pushing for a view, I left with the food, eager to share my findings.

"What's it like?" said Cathole next to me, wishing for once he'd been table monitor.

"It moves about – like jelly," I said.

"Must be lime jelly then," said Darke.

"And there's something black in the middle that keeps changing shape," I said.

"Could be a tadpole," said Cathole, who'd had a lot of frogspawn in his pond that year.

"It was toppling out of the eye like a slinky when I arrived, but went back up at the last minute," I said. "I thought it was going to drop into the fish."

"Probably didn't like the look of it," said Cathole.

"Or the vegetables," said Butlin. "Don't blame it. They're boiled to buggery."

From L to P came raucous laughter as Lewniham told them what he'd seen at the hatches. He'd noticed Dead-Eye's head begin to bow and had taken full advantage of her dispirited condition to get extra portions for his table, more than enough to cater for Lee's voracious appetite.

Meanwhile, Lee had been watching and waiting. He told us afterwards he'd been sucking a blue gobstopper in the queue outside until it was roughly what he thought would fit Dead-Eye's socket, then moved the sticky object to his blazer pocket. As Lewniham came past on his way from the hatches, he'd seized his opportunity.

"I say old fellow," he said, pointing to our table. "Aren't they supposed to get theirs first?"

It's true that Lewniham *had* barged in at the front of the pudding queue, but being in Dead-Eye's good books he'd got away with it.

"Shut up, you lardy cunt," he said to Lee. But in the second it took Lewniham to follow Lee's pointing hand, Lee had dropped his time bomb deep in the semolina pudding. Le Clerc was the only one who saw this, and told us what happened next. Having hived off an extra large dollop of raspberry jam for himself before passing the small aluminium jug down the table, Lewniham stirred the semolina. At first he'd appeared to treat the object deep in the bowl as yet another lump, scooping it to the edge with the others, presumably to put on Lee's plate. Then his eyes lit up. Covered in semolina it was hard to tell, but the object was circular and solid and Lewniham, who must have been convinced it was Dead-Eye's missing eye, quietly tucked the sticky ball into a sticky, grey handkerchief from his pocket.

Before it was time to do so, he stood up and walked to the hatches with the empty containers. The canteen quietened as he drew attention to himself, but he didn't seem to care. This would be his crowning moment; he'd be eternally in Dead-Eye's favour. We watched her raise her head and smile meekly – which with an eye that wouldn't settle was more like the grin of a mad woman.

"Cheer up," we heard him say boldly, reaching into his pocket. "I've got something that'll make your day."

Dead-Eye took a step back as he offered the grubby package. Peeling back the corners of the gooey cloth she saw her missing eye, caked with setting semolina but intact. Her haddock eye remained restless, but the real, china blue one at last started twinkling again.

"Lewniham, how can I possibly thank you enough?" she said, moving to the sink to wash off the semolina.

No doubt he had a few ideas but would keep them for another day. Right now he had pudding to eat before Lee got his hands on it.

"Aaargh!" The scream permeated the canteen and shot two hundred yards down the street outside. Spoons stopped scraping as Dead-Eye's head loomed through the hatches, the haddock eye zinging to and fro at twice its earlier speed.

"You - what d'you think you're doing?" she bellowed towards Lewniham's table. "Do you think that's funny?"

Lewniham looked around, as if unclear whom she was addressing. He tried hiding, first behind Le Clerc then Midgley who offered little cover, but one by one the boys ducked down leaving him directly in Dead-Eye's line of sight.

"Yes – you!" she screeched, pointing at the isolated Lewniham. She was back to her former self, and her tone terrified him. "What's your game? Come here, you! Do you *hear* me?"

* * *

"Oi! What's your game?" a man is shouting. Through the fogged windows I see traffic moving. Car horns are blaring, articulated lorries roaring by alarmingly close. A hard-to-follow comedy has replaced Eddie Mair.

"Sod off!" I mouth at the man. Clearly motorway spirit doesn't last like Dunkirk.

I head on to the Trossachs, where no doubt Cathole and Cornichon will remind me what became of Lee and Lewniham. Or we'll think up a suitable ending.

REBEKAH DUNNE is nearing the end of her final year studying English at BCU, and has always dreamed of being a published writer. She loves reading children's books, in which she finds far more scope for the imagination, and this has influenced her own writing. Even if you are an adult she hopes you will still enjoy the results.

Turtles for Christmas
by Rebekah Dunne

Friday

Dear Diary,

GUESS WHAT? GUESS WHAT? GUESS WHAT? GUESS WHAT?

Mummy and Daddy brought me the new KINECT and it's not even Christmas yet! I've wanted it for ages but Mummy kept saying it was too expensive, but when I got home today it was just there! I wanted to start playing on it right away but Mummy said that I had to have tea first. She made Dino chicken nuggets with chips and BEANS instead of peas! It's the bestest food in the world!

Daddy and me wolfed it down and raced to the Kinect. I got there first. We played for ages and I won every single game, except for all the girly games. Daddy was rubbish! Mummy even let us eat ice-cream in the living room! I had 2 scoops of all 3 flavours and Daddy had 3 of each! Epic!

I didn't go to bed on time because we had to get to level 4 on the team game (we had to switch to the team game because Daddy kept getting KOed and it made him growchie grouchy.)

Today has been sick! But I've got to go to bed because the faster I do, the sooner it'll be Saturday! No school! Yes! The WHOLE day playing the Kinect!

Saturday

Dear Diary,

You will never guess where I've been all day? No, not on the Kinect, I only got 2 hours on that. (2 epic hours.)

Mummy and Daddy took me to the Sea-life centre!!!

It must be because I'm doing awesomely at school.

YEAH!!!!

I saw sharks and turtles and I even got to hold a star-fish! It felt all weird. I asked Mummy if we could take a turtle home and she said that if I really wanted one and I was really good, then Santa might bring me one! How awesome would that be? I want the one with the stripe on its head, so I've already wrote it on my Christmas list and drawn a picture, just in case.

Anyway they even had a cinema where the Dolphins jump out the screen and splash water on you! It went in my mouth. YUK! It was so gross that Mummy had to buy me an ice-lolly just to get the taste away. (Or so she thinks.)

Daddy didn't look like he was having fun but Mummy said that he was just tired. Mummy and me had a great time. She brought me a turtle teddy from the gift shop so that I can get ready for if Santa brings me a *real* one. I hope it's got a stripe on its head.

Ooh I should put a holiday to Sea-world on my Christmas list! If I keep getting good marks at school I'll probably get it too.

Sunday

Dear Diary,

Mummy and Daddy woke me up this morning yelling at each other. I came downstairs to try and stop them but they didn't even notice me at first. They just kept screaming. Mummy's voice goes really high when she's mad. It's usually funny but this time it was scary. I had to cover my ears because it was making me cry.

They noticed me then.

Mummy picked me up and took me back to bed. She wouldn't tell me why they were being mean to each other. She said that they were just being silly and not to worry about it. They have had fights in the past but never like this. I don't get it, I thought I was being good? What's there to fight about?

After Mummy left Daddy came in with some Lucky Charms.

We aren't usually allowed them because Mummy says they are too expensive and make your teeth rot, but Daddy said it's alright just this once, as a treat.

Only Daddy took me to church. Mummy couldn't come because she had to make a very special tea for me. Spaghetti and meatballs! My almost-favourite. I love sluuuuurping my spaghetti up so that it flicks my nose! And it's fun when you don't think the spaghetti will ever end. It's the most fun you can have at tea-time.

I saved a meatball to give to turtle teddy (I think I'll be ready for the real thing very soon).

Monday

Dear Diary,

Not seen Daddy since I came home from school. I waited and waited for him to come and play on the Kinect with me and it was so boooring. I kept asking Mummy when he would be home and after I asked the 4th time she told me to just go and play by myself. She was so mean. We had jacket potatoes with cheesy beans for tea and she was quiet for the longest time. She didn't even ask me where my school report was.

I took it out and gave it to her anyway and she just put it on the side instead of reading it straight away like she usually does. What have I done wrong?

I started playing the Kinect but Mummy said that it was too loud and to turn it off. I tried just turning it down but that made her mad and she sent me to my room. It's not fair. I didn't even do anything wrong. Not really.

She made me go to bed really early as well. 8 o'clock! And Daddy still wasn't back.

Tuesday

Dear Diary,

I woke up today and Daddy was sitting on my bed holding more Lucky Charms but this time I didn't want them. I yelled and told him that I waited ALL day for him to play Kinect with me but he didn't show. He wasn't even there to say goodnight to me and where *was* he anyway? He had the world's most crappiest excuse ever too! He said that he had to work late. It's not fair.

I didn't eat my Lucky Charms. Daddy tried and tried but I just crossed my arms and clamped my mouth shut and kept shaking my head. Daddy said that Santa wouldn't bring me my Turtle if I wasn't good, but I don't even care so there!

He left in the end and my Lucky Charms were just sat there getting soggy. It wasn't *really* fair to let them go to waste. I mean it's not *their* fault that Daddy is using them as a way to make me forget what he did is it? So I ate them as quickly as I could and hid the plate under my bed so that Daddy wouldn't see. They were really tasty.

School was so booooring I couldn't wait to be home but Daddy was there and he had cooked more Dino nuggets, chips and beans. I just went straight to my room and slammed the door shut. Daddy came in not long after and reminded me about how I accidently spilt Ribena on the white carpet and how mad he was but he still forgave me. Then he left.

And he was right. It wasn't *his* fault that he had to work, was it? And maybe if I hadn't been so mad at him we could have played together on the Kinect tonight, instead of being sat in here bored.

I stayed in my room for a little longer to prove my point then went down to the dinner table and ate my nuggets. I think it made him happy. I don't know how happy he will be if he finds the cereal bowl under my bed though.

It was time for bed almost straight after tea. But Daddy promised that we would play on the Kinect tomorrow after school.

Wednesday

Dear Diary,

I couldn't wait to get home from school and guess who was in the living room with the Kinect already set up? Daddy! I guess he has learnt his lesson. We played and played right up till dinner (yukky chicken stew) and then played and played after dinner too! It was fan-dabby-dosie and he said that we might even be able to do it again tomorrow!

When I was getting ready for bed I saw Mummy pass my room and she was wearing a dress. A nice dress! I asked if she and Daddy were going out but she said that it was only her going.

Without Daddy?

What was she doing?

Maybe she has to go to a meeting with Santa Claus?

Daddy put me to bed but he wasn't as jolly as he usually is. He rushed through the bed-time story and tucked me in a little bit rougher than usual. He forgot to tuck Turtle teddy in with me (I will have to give him a name eventually.) I called him back in and he almost THREW teddy at me. But when he was about to leave he came back and tucked him in properly and said sorry and kissed me on my head.

After he had left I held turtle teddy in the air and tried to think of a name that suits him.

Bobby. No.

Allen. No.

Maybe something beginning with a T?

Theodore? Like in the Chipmunks? Nah, that's kids stuff.

Tiny Timmy Turtle? No. That's too *many* T's.

Trevor? Like in Harry Potter? Yes!!!!! Trevor Turtle! Tomorrow I will have to baptise him with his new name in the bath tub. That's what Steve from Sunday School said you have to do, or else the name doesn't count.

I'll let you know how it goes tomorrow.

Thursday

Dear Diary,

I couldn't have a bath this morning so used the sink instead. Trevor really enjoyed being baptised, actually he wanted to be baptised twice! I can't wait to baptise a *real* turtle! Mummy came in when I was drying him off and started shouting to stop messing around and get ready for school. Daddy heard her yelling and started to shout from the kitchen to leave me alone, but that only made Mummy madder!

School was really boooring as usual and I couldn't wait for home-time. Mummy was late which was really weird. The teacher said to stay in reception until she gets here and the receptionist lady gave me some milk and a biscuit. Yummy.

I tried to think of why Mummy might have been late. Maybe she's meeting Santa again! I did just get an awesome score in a spelling test.

Or maybe she is meeting someone else?

Someone top secret.

A *spy?*

Maybe Mummy wants a new job as a spy.

That would be *so* cool.

Then when I grow up, I can be a spy too!

I'm clever enough.

And sneaky enough.

Yeah. That would be cool.

A lifetime had gone by when Mummy rushed in and grabbed me by the hand and said sorry and thank you to the receptionist and rushed me to the car.

Maybe she was being followed!

I asked her why she was late but all she said was that she and Daddy had to sort something out. That's pretty boring. I tried to find out more but she just told me to be quiet.

We picked up a bag of fish and chips on the way home and Mummy said that I could eat it in my room! I'm not usually allowed food into my room (except when Daddy sometimes sneaks a plate in for me. *He* would make a cool spy). I grabbed my plate when it was ready and raced to my room before she changed her mind. But as soon as I shut my door I heard Mummy and Daddy trying to argue quietly. But they weren't *that* quiet. Trevor didn't like the yelling either and I had to put his hands (I wonder what you call them for a turtle?) over his ears.

In the end I just got into bed and put the pillows over our heads and closed my eyes.

Friday

Dear Diary,

Mummy slept late today which means that all of us slept late. We rushed to school again but they don't get that my legs are shorter than theirs.

It's the last day of school before the Christmas holidays. I never thought this day would come! No more books! No more tests! Just the Kinect and Christmas presents!

I got into trouble for not doing my homework but I don't care. What are they going to do...give me more homework? They tried to keep me back for 10 minutes after school because they're mean. Like homework really matters anyway. But when Mummy came she wasn't having any of it. She said that in future they would have to keep me in at break times because she doesn't have time to wait around. I wish she had said that they couldn't keep me in *at all*.

I spat my tongue out at them as we left.

That showed them.

No Daddy when we got home again. I asked Mummy if she would play with me but she said that we could both sit and play and starve or she could cook tea for us and then clean up the house so that we didn't have to live in a swamp. I wish I hadn't asked in the end because she sent me to my room to tidy it too. I haven't even done anything wrong! Well, except the homework thing. She said that it was a pigsty and that if Nanny ever came over and saw it she would be horrified.

It took forever to clean and was so booooring! I even had to go back to cleaning after tea! (Yukky, yukky stew.) I wish we had a dog so that I could have slipped him some.

It's finally done but now its bed time and Daddy still isn't home. He probably has to work late again. He has had to work late a lot lately.

Saturday

Dear Diary,

Daddy wasn't here when I got up and Mummy was in a bad mood again. Why is everyone so grouchy? It's nearly Christmas! She sent me to my cousin's house to spend the day while she did her "chores". I usually go with her to do her chores...maybe she is going to meet up with Santa about my Christmas presents and that's why I can't go with her. Or maybe it's another spy's meeting?

My cousin is older than me and she thinks that she knows way more than I do so I was very bored waiting for Mummy to get back. She likes watching what she calls "big girl" programmes on TV, but all that means is that people stand around and talk rather than do anything fun or exciting. And she hates computer games and the Wii AND the Kinect AND she likes doing jigsaw puzzles! That's boring! If that's what it's like to be grown-up then I want to be a kid for the rest of my life, thank you very much.

She was really horrible to me as well. She asked if Mummy and Daddy had sorted things out yet. I asked her what she was talking about and she said that her Mum said that my Mummy and Daddy didn't love each other anymore and were going to get a divorce. I asked her what a divorce was and she said it meant that they're not going to live together anymore and that I would soon have a new Mummy and Daddy.

I called her a liar and an idiot and said she didn't know what she was talking about. But she said that she was older and knew a lot more than me. She asked me if I had heard them fighting and going from being really nice, to hardly talking in the same minute. When I didn't answer she got this really disgusting smile on her face and said "Told you so."

So guess what I did? I pulled and pulled her hair until she cried. That will teach her!

When Mummy got back and found out what I had done (my cousin's such a snitch) she took me home right away and made me get into bed and said that I can forget Santa bringing me a Turtle for Christmas. But she's already gone to see Santa, before she knew what I had done, so he wouldn't know anyway... would he?

What if the elves tell on me?

It's not fair. It's not my fault that my cousin is a horrid, smelly old girl!!!

Santa will understand, I'm going to write and explain everything.

I'll practise what I write first, just in case. We learnt how to write a letter in school the other day, so this one should be good.

Sunday

Dear Santa,

I haven't got a lot of time to write this because I have to go to church in a bit, but I thought I would try and clear up some of the stuff that the elves might be telling you. Oh it's Ruben by the way (in case you didn't know.)

The elves have probably told you that I pulled my cousin's hair and made her cry and yes, that is true but you don't know what she did to deserve it. She told me that my Mummy and Daddy were going to get a divorce and that they didn't love each other anymore and that they wanted a new Mummy and Daddy for me. Isn't that mean! Doesn't she deserve to be punished?

Can you understand now why I did what I did? Because I really,

really, REALLY want my Turtle for Christmas.

I'm sorry that I did it, but she deserved it. I bet you think that I'm right too.

I gotta go to church now. Please, Please still bring me my Turtle.

Yours sinseerely sincerely,

Ruben.

Monday

Dear Diary,

Daddy pulled me out of bed this morning and said that he had to work from home today because Mummy wouldn't be around. He didn't even make me breakfast. He just said that I knew where the cereal was and that I was big enough to start taking care of myself. I felt so proud, until I dropped the milk carton on to the floor and it went everywhere and Daddy yelled at me. He told me to play on my Kinect and to be quiet while he worked. After aaaages I asked where Mummy was and he said that she was sorting some things out and wouldn't be home tonight either. But what was she sorting out? And how long would she be gone for? He wouldn't answer any of my questions. He just told me to go to my room and do my homework while he tried to find something for us to have for tea.

I wonder what she's sorting out.

Maybe it's code for something.

Maybe she's been Mummy-napped!

Daddy was busy in the kitchen and when he came out he said that we would have to go out for something to eat. Maybe a McDonalds! I put my shoes on as quickly as I could and stood by the door while Daddy got ready. It takes him so long. He's like a girl!

I had a happy meal and wolfed it down. I asked if I could have some ice-cream and he even gave me the money to get it myself like a real grown-up.

He was being really nice to me.

Suspiciously nice.

Maybe he knows where Mummy has been held hostage.

When we got home Daddy sat me down on the sofa and said he had something to tell me. He said that he and Mummy loved me very much but that they were going to live in different homes. I didn't bother asking anything else. I just said I wanted to go to bed.

I wish Mummy *had* been mummy-napped. It's better than being an Orphan.

Tuesday

Dear Diary,

Happy Christmas eve-eve. Not that there's much to be happy about today. Trevor and me talked a lot this morning and we came up with some really good questions to ask Daddy:

What is going to happen with Christmas?

Where will my turtle live if Santa does bring one?

Does Santa bring presents for Orphans?

One of the worst parts about all of this is that I will have to admit that my stinky-smelly cousin was right all along.

I went looking for Daddy in the living room, but MUMMY was there instead! She made us pancakes for breakfast! She put bananas on them to make them healthy and I was going to push them to one side, but then I thought that if I was naughty she might leave again, so I ate them first as quickly as I could so that I could finish with my pancakes.

Then Mummy said that if I got my hat and gloves on then she would take me to the park! It was brill! I even got ALL the way across the monkey bars without *any* help! It must have been my superhero breakfast.

And then...you will never guess what we did...we went to the cinema to see Puss in Boots! It was awesome! The best day ever!

Wednesday

Dear Diary,

Merry Christmas Eve! I've pushed my bean-bag in front of my door because I am about to undertake very top-secret stuff. I'm serious. No one can know what's happening in here. I'm making Mummy and Daddy's Christmas presents. And I have a sneaky idea. A plan to get Mummy and Daddy back together. I know that yesterday was great but it won't last forever and I don't want to be an Orphan.

So if I make Mummy and Daddy something to do together, then they will remember why they love each other. (YUK) I think that this will take me the whole day so I'm going to get going and I'll let you know how it goes tomorrow.

Thursday

Dear Diary,

Happy Christmas!!! I haven't got long because I have to go to Mummy's soon but I finished their present last night. It's a top of the range, awesome, amazing, one of a kind game scoring board...sort of. It turns out that I didn't have all the stuff that they said I would need off Art Attack...like cardboard and paint and stuff. But this big paper (I stuck loads of normal paper together) looks epic now that I have drawn reindeer on it and put their names on.

Oh Mummy just beeped the horn so I've got to go...but you will never guess what Santa brought me...A TURTLE!!! A little brother for Trevor! It even has a stripe on its head! I'm so glad that he decided to bring me one after all! I guess I am a good boy really. It must have been the school report.

Dear Diary,

Santa left a turtle at Mommy's house too!! I must be a REALLY good boy. So now I have one of each kind! A boy AND a girl! I've got to baptise and name them now. It's so exciting!

But the day didn't go like I wanted it to. I gave Mummy and Daddy their present but they weren't as excited as last year. But we all gave it a go. Turns out that tournaments don't last very long and when it was done they just said thanks to me and put it away. They didn't even seem to care.

We all had Christmas dinner together but then Daddy and I went home and Mummy stayed at her new house. It's the worst Christmas ever! We usually play games like truth or dare and twister and things like that on Christmas night. But instead Daddy just put a film on and it was crappy.

I've come to bed early because I want to introduce Trevor to his new brother and because it's really boring out there tonight.

Friday

Dear Diary,

Daddy made me get up early AGAIN today because it's Mummy's day to have me. I guess this is how it's going to be from now on. Mummy or Daddy. I mean, don't get me wrong the extra presents and special treatment are nice but it's not the same.

I would trade all of the turtles in all of the world just to have my Mummy and Daddy living in the same house again.

I'm kind of like Peter Pan in a way though. And my Turtles are like my Tinkerbell...only cooler. In fact I named the boy turtle Mr. Smee and I named the girl turtle Tiger-Lilly, so it's almost like I really AM Peter Pan.

I'm sure I will get used to things soon but I still can't figure out what went wrong. Why it's my parents that had to split up and not someone else's. Not smelly Halle's parents. They're still married. What's different about her Mummy and Daddy and mine?

Does it have something to do with me?

Is it my fault?

Did they really ever love each other?

Do they really love other people?

What happens if Mummy or Daddy *do* love other people?

What happens to me?

I still have so many questions. Watch this space for any answers that I can figure out.

GEORGINA SHACKELL GREEN is a second year English student hoping for some sort of career in some sort of writing. Or something related. She's not too sure yet... Hopefully her Third Year will give her some insight.

Bittersweet
by Georgina Green

Arrive late. Not for fashion but to avoid
the Noah's ark style entry.
And pretend you don't notice
the red, velvet (empty) seat beside you.

Try to blink back the blurring in your eyes
and then when you can't,
thank the beautiful woman who's passing a tissue.
Remember to tell her they are tears of joy
and you've never been more proud.

Watch the people around as they clap and hug and smile.
Copy. This is how you're supposed to act.
Today is still a day of celebration,
You should be happy. Don't think about the missing piece.

CHERRELLE HIGGS is currently finishing her Masters in Writing at Birmingham City University. Her love of theatre began at a young age when she took centre stage and this lead her to develop her own plays. Influenced by the likes of Sarah Kane, her work pushes the boundaries of traditional theatre. *Inside* is a complex play that demonstrates the outlandish world that Cherrelle is keen to explore in her playwriting.

Inside
by Cherrelle Higgs

Main Characters:

Stacey: 25 years old, appears 'normal'. We learn she was in a car accident and her father died. She believes she is grieving and shouldn't be in Longbourgh Hospital. She's 'not like them'.

Matt: 25 years old. Angry and physically aggressive when things don't go his way. Everyone stays clear except for Lily who does anything he says.

Lily: 25 years old. Resorts to her child like state to cope with day to day life and which makes her very gullible.

Tim: 25 years old. He will not speak. He communicates through pictures and he keeps writing the same numbers over and over again. He mumbles and whispers things that we can't quite make out.

Bev: 25 years old. She is on suicide watch as any chance she gets she will try and take her own life. She doesn't want to live anymore and blames the nurses for keeping her here. She is paranoid and anxious.

Minor Characters:

Mrs Cooper/Mom: Late 50's, immaculately dressed. She cannot believe her daughter is in a place like Longbourgh and is having a difficult time coming to terms with her diagnosis.

Psychologist: Male, early 30's. Dressed in a suit carrying a briefcase.

Here we are

Speakers: *(Spoken softly and slowly.)* Welcome to Longbourgh hospital. Visiting hours are from 1.30pm to 3pm. You are reminded to keep at a distance from patients and keep sudden movements to a minimum. In the case of an emergency a red light will flash. Please follow orders.

> *All patients have identical scars on their faces. Tim is drawing pictures of clocks showing 7 o'clock, the date 2/12/09 and a cross. Lily is rolling around on the floor and banging into Matt. Matt is pushing her away whilst getting increasingly annoyed, but Lily thinks it's funny. Stacey is sitting at the back overlooking all the other patients.*

Matt: Lily, stop it!

Lily: Just play, Matt.

Matt: I don't want to play.

Lily: Yes, you do. *(She stops rolling into him.)* OK, punch me as hard as you can. *(Lifts top showing stomach.)* Right here, go on.

Matt: Don't tempt me.

Lily: Come on Matt, it's your best game.

Matt: Later. Go and play with mute over there.

Lily: *(Upset.)* But he's no fun.

Matt: *(Angrily.)* I don't care.

> *Lily makes her way over to Tim.*

Lily: Tim, do you want to play?

> *Tim is whispering and ignoring Lily.*

Lily: Tim. Tim! *(Pause.)* It's not nice to ignore me. Tim! *(She turns her back on him as if she is ignoring him, then turns* *around.)* Can I draw too? You've got to share, it's good to share.

> *Lily takes a piece of paper. Tim stops drawing and whispering and stares angrily at Lily. Lily takes a pencil. Tim snatches his pencil and paper back and covers them with his body, frantically whispering and looking angrily at Lily. Lily slowly moves back to Matt and pushes him, trying to get his attention.*

Stacey: *(To audience.)* I shouldn't be here. Come on, just look at them. I'm the only sane one in here. Does it look like there's anything wrong with me? I should be sitting where you're sitting.

> *Stacey points at an audience member and walks towards them.*

Speaker: Guests are reminded to keep at a safe distance from all patients.

Stacey: *(Laughs.)* They're warning you now. They're warning you about me. What do they think I'm going to do to you, there's nothing wrong with me.

> *Stacey goes to grab an audience member. White light flashes. All patients stand in line. They pick up a cup in front of them named 'Cocaine', 'Amphetamines' and 'Cannabis'. They simultaneously empty the contents into their mouth. They then stand there and open their mouths showing it is empty and return to places.*

Stacey: *(Walking backwards to the chair.)* He's the one you should be scared of.

> *Stacey points at Matt. Matt punches Lily as she keeps pushing him, trying to get his attention.*

Lily: Owww, Matt! *(Going to cry.)* That hurt.

Matt: No, it didn't.

Lily: I'm telling/

Matt: *(Gets Lily in a headlock.)* / Who you going to tell, huh? *(Tightens grip.)* Who you going to tell?

Lily: *(Gasping.)* No one, no one.

> *Matt lets go and starts laughing. Lily holds her neck and then starts laughing with Matt. All characters begin laughing. Then silence.*

Speaker: Visitor in visiting room 1. Could *(static sound)* please enter visiting room 1.

Lily: *(Excited.)* Did they just say my name? They said my name didn't they? A visitor for me? I haven't had a visitor since yesterday.

> *As Lily walks towards the back of the room, Mom walks in. She is wearing a nametag saying 'Mrs Cooper'. She stands in the centre of the space whilst all other patients sit as if watching the meeting.*

Lily: *(Running to Mom.)* Mom! *(Hugging her.)*

Mom: Ok. *(Trying to get her off.)* Ok, get off.

Lily: I've missed you.

Stacey: *(Mimicking Lily.)* I've missed you.

Mom: Mmm.

Lily: *(Playful.)* Mom?

Mom: I've told you to stop calling me that.

Lily: *(Long pause.)* Lets play hide and seek. *(Excited.)* I'll count. One... two... three... *(Peeks through hands.)*... four...five...six... 7,8,9,10. *(Mom hasn't moved. Lily excitedly takes hands away.)* Found you. *(Laughs.)* Ok, now I'll hide. Count Mom, count.

Lily runs around the empty space looking for a place to hide.

Mom: Stop it.

Lily: I can't hear you counting.

Mom: Stop it! *(Lily stands still.)* I can't do this!

Lily: It's not a hard game.

Mom: You're a grown woman. You shouldn't be acting like a two year old.

Lily: *(Confused.)* What?

Mom: Let me out! I can't do this.

Lily: But mom...

Mom exits. All characters resume their places.

Matt: *(To Lily.)* What happened?

Lily: She didn't want to play.

A buzzer sounds. Bev enters, scared and unsure of her surroundings.

Matt: *(Walks over to Bev.)* What do we have here? Whoa! What do you think you're doing? *(He grabs her neck.)* Who do you think you are, walking all over my space? You're not welcome! Stay over there.

Matt pushes Bev and she falls. She then sits holding herself tightly.

Stacey: Not another one. They can't keep doing this. We've got no room for anymore. *(To Bev.)* Who are you? What are you here for? *(Walks to her, grabs her arm revealing the cuts on her arm.)* Oh, you're a right nut job. *(To audience, Grabs Bev's arm.)* Look, they are keeping me here with this. It's not fair I haven't done anything.

Stacey pushes Bev who falls into Matt. Stacey storms to her chair.

Matt: *(To Bev.)* Was I not clear? Why are you all up in my space? You need to learn very quickly. I'm not someone you want to get on the wrong side of.

Bev: I'm sorry I/

Matt: /No! You're not sorry, but you will be.

A loud beeping noise is heard. Stacey walks over to Matt assertively.

Matt: Oh, come on, I was joking. I was joking.

Stacey: You can't keep doing this to me!

The psychologist enters. Stacey sits Matt down and along with all the other characters, sits in a corner of the stage watching the meeting.

Matt: I didn't do anything, so I don't know why you're here.

Psychologist: I believe there has been some confrontation between you and Bev.

Matt: No. *(Pause. Calm.)* I like her, she's alright.

Psychologist: There has been reports of threats made, is that correct?

Matt: She couldn't threaten me /I'd break her neck.

The psychologist raises his eyebrows.

Matt: What? She wants to die anyway.

Psychologist: And you think you should be the one/ to...

Matt: /Look, Doc. She came in my space. I don't like that.

Psychologist: You don't like people getting too close?

Matt: Don't start with all that psychological crap.

Psychologist: Why are you feeling so angry?

Matt: *(Angrily.)* I'm not angry. *(Bangs table.)*

Psychologist: Is this because of Mr Cooper?

Matt: Don't bring him into this.

Psychologist: This is not going to get better until you talk about him.

Matt: I don't want to talk about it.

Psychologist: That accident wasn't your fault.

Matt: Stop it!

Psychologist: There was nothing you could have done.

Matt: *(Picks up chair and goes to throw it at the psychologist.)* Stop it!

Stacey: *(With urgency.)* Matt what are you doing?

Matt puts the chair down and goes to his original place. The psychologist leaves. Bev sits scared in her corner of the room holding herself tightly. Tim continues drawing. Lily sits staring at Matt. Stacey looks on.

Lily: You look mad.

Matt: *(Pushes Lily.)* Just leave me alone.

Lily goes over to Bev.

Lily: What's your name?

Bev tries to move away from Lily.

Bev: Bev.

Lily: I'm Lily. Matt just likes to play naughty games, don't be scared. *(Pause.)* What's that? *(Points to Bev's neck).*

Bev: It's nothing. *(Covers her scars up.)*

Lily: I've got that too. *(Shows her an identical scar on her neck.)*

Bev: *(Pause.)* What did you do?

Lily: Matt bet me that my sock couldn't hold me to the ceiling, but mine are strong. *(Pause.)* Your socks must be strong too.

Bev: I didn't … didn't use socks.

Lily: *(Interested.)* What did you use?

Bev: *(Quietly.)* Rope.

Stacey: *(As Bev.)* Rope.

Lily: Wow. I didn't think of that. Who bet you?

Bev: What?

Lily: Who bet you that rope couldn't hold you?

Bev: No one. No one bet me. I did it because I wanted to.

Lily: *(Shocked, excited.)* Why?

Bev: I don't want to talk about it.

Lily: *(Upset.)* You don't want to play either. Matt!

Bev: No. Ok.

Lily: Why?

Bev: The only person who understood me and really cared died right in front of me. *(Long pause.)* You're not going to tell anyone are you?

Lily: Cross my heart and hope to die.

Bev: He died right in front of me. There was nothing I could do. I tried. I tried everything. I was young. I didn't know what to do. *(Upset.)*

Lily: /He died?

Stacey: *(As Lily.)* / He died?

Bev: Yeah.

Lily: *(Long pause.)* Everyone has to die. That's what my mom told me.

Stacey sees Matt alone, and sees opportunity to talk to him.

Stacey: Hey Matt. Matt!

Matt: What's your problem?

Stacey: Shh! They'll hear you.

Matt: What?

Stacey: Don't let them get to you /I can…

Matt: *(Angry.)* /Just leave me alone Stacey.

Stacey: I can help you.

Matt: No one can help me.

Stacey: Do you really want to be here for the rest of your life?

Matt: Of course I don't.

Stacey: We need to get out of here. There's nothing wrong with us, we shouldn't be here.

Matt: We can't do anything without them seeing.

Stacey: That's why we have to be like them. *(Looks at audience.)* When they all leave, we can get out with them. We just have to time it properly. Staying here is making us crazy. They're not helping us, they're making us worse. We have to go, we have to get out and go back to the real world.

Matt: I'm in.

Stacey: We just have to convince the rest now.

Matt: What? You said nothing about them coming.

Stacey: We can't do this without them.

Matt: It's not going to work. They deserve to be here anyway.

Stacey: If they don't come, we'll ALL be stuck here.

Matt: They'll just hold us up.

Stacey: *(Assertively.)* We're taking them with us Matt.

> *White light flashes. All patients stand in line. They pick up a cup in front of them named 'Cocaine', 'Amphetamines' and 'Cannabis'. They simultaneously empty the contents into their mouth. They then stand there and open their mouths showing it is empty and return to places. Bev takes the cup and tries to cut her right arm. All patients hold their right arm in pain.*

Lily: Owwww!

Stacey: Bev, what are you doing?

Matt: *(To Bev.)* Oi.

> *Takes cup off Bev and throws it.*

Bev: Look, I don't want any trouble. I haven't done /anything...

Matt: /Shut up! *(Whispers.)* We're all getting out of here and for some reason we've got to take you with us.

Bev: I can't, I/

Matt: /I didn't ask you, you're coming. Be ready after last pill.

Bev: Last pill?

Matt: I didn't stutter. We're finally saying goodbye to this place.

Bev: but I...I...

Matt: You're coming! If you tell anyone about this, you'll wish you never met me.

Bev: What if they catch us? I don't want to stay here forever.

Matt: Shh! They'll hear you. I'm trying so hard to keep my hands to myself right now.

Bev: *(Getting very anxious.)* They're always watching, how can we do this? We can't get... We won't be able to/

Matt: *(Aggressively, covering her mouth.)* /I'm telling you, we are all going to do this. Do not mess this up.

Bev nods her head.

Matt: *(Rubbing his right arm.)* Now don't try anything else.

Lily: What are you talking to her for?

Matt: I'm not.

Lily: You did, you just did.

Matt: Jealous?

Lily: No, no I'm going to talk to... *(Looks around.)* Stacey.

Matt: Go on then.

Lily: Yeah I will.

Lily goes over to Stacey

Lily: Hi Stacey.

Stacey: Hi. *(Long pause.)* What do you want?

Lily: Nothing.

Lily stands there fidgeting.

Stacey: Actually, Lily, come over here, I've got a game to play.

Lily: *(Excited)* Oh yeah, really?

Lily looks to see if Matt is watching.

Stacey: Ok sit there. You have to guess how many fingers I'm holding up.

Lily: OK!

> *Stacey holds up four fingers.*

Lily: Four.

Stacey: Lucky guess.

> *Stacey holds up nine fingers.*

Lily: Nine.

Stacey: *(Confused.)* Can you see them?

Lily: No, they're behind your back, you're not invisible.

> *Stacey holds up one finger.*

Lily: One.

> *Stacey changes in quick succession to three, seven, zero.*

Lily: *(As Stacey changes.)* Three, seven, zero.

Stacey: How are you doing that? You're like, psychic or something.

Lily: *(Laughs)* I know.

Stacey: Well, do you want to hear a secret?

Lily: Yeah.

Stacey: Well, me and Matt have got a game we're playing later. Do you want to play?

Lily: Yeah!

Stacey: It's a big girl's game.

Lily: I'm a big girl!

Stacey: I know. That's why I think you should play. Do you want to go outside?

Lily: I'm not allowed outside anymore. They banned me when

Matt tried to bury me in the sand. He's not allowed out either.

Stacey: No, I mean outside the gates, where they don't let us go.

Lily: I've always wanted to go there!

Stacey: Shh! They'll hear you.

Lily puts her hand over her mouth.

Stacey: Ok, so…We have been kept hostage in here and the doctors are the criminals. We have to escape or they'll kill us. *(Lily gasps.)* So we have to sneak past them to get our freedom.

Lily: This is going to be the best game ever!

Stacey: You have to be quiet though and don't tell anyone. It's our secret.

Lily: Yeah, our secret.

Stacey nods to Matt signalling Lily is on board with their plan. Matt walks over to Tim.

Matt: *(To Tim.)* Well, I know *you're* not going to say anything to them. *(Tim continues to draw.)* We are all going to get out of this dump, and we've got to take you with us. /Are you listening to me? *(Snatches pencil.)*

Stacey: *(As Matt to audience.)* /Are you listening to me?

Matt: *(To Tim.)* That's rude. Now, we are leaving this nut house and you're coming with us. We're doing you a favour. No need to thank us. If you mess this up…

Matt breaks Tim's pencil and begins to walk away. Tim holds the broken pencil pieces in his hand and looks distraught. He then angrily lunges at Matt.

Matt: What do you think you're doing! Get off me! Get off me!

Stacey rushes over and tries to separate them.

Stacey: What's going on?!

Matt: *(To Tim.)* You're going to regret that!

Stacey: Stop it, they'll hear you.

Tim gets out of Stacey's grip and continues to draw pictures.

Stacey: *(To Matt.)* What happened?

Matt: I didn't do anything. He just went crazy.

Stacey: Did you tell him?

Matt: Yeah, before he threw himself at me.

Stacey: So everyone's on board?

Matt: Yeah, we got everyone.

Stacey: Well, it's all go after last pills tonight. *(Stacey picks up a piece of broken pencil and looks at it distraught like Tim did.)* Try not to get into any more trouble.

Matt: He came at me!

Here we go

White light flashes. All patients stand in line. They pick up a cup in front of them named 'Cocaine', 'Amphetamines' and 'Cannabis'. They simultaneously empty the contents into their mouth. They then stand there and open their mouths showing it is empty and return to places.

Stacey: It's time. Let's go.

They all go and hide behind an audience member. Bev runs around the stage looking for somewhere to hide. She sits on stage rocking.

Bev: *(Repeats.)* I can't do this. I can't go. They'll find me.

Stacey: What is she doing?

Matt: *(Angry.)* I'll get her.

Red light flashes.

Speaker: *(Calm, slowly.)* All guests, please remain calm. Everything is under control. I repeat everything is under control.

Matt: They know!

Lily: *(To audience.)* We're hostages, help us.

Stacey: RUN!

They all run around the stage frantically looking for a way out. They then simultaneously fall to the ground holding their heads in pain, screaming.

Blackout.

Lights up. All characters are lying motionless on stage.

Speakers: *(Softly, slowly.)* Patient is no longer a risk. Visiting hours cease in 15 minutes.

Characters begin to wake up holding their heads.

Stacey: What was that?

Lily: I don't want to be a hostage anymore.

Matt: Them fucking doctors. How did they do that?

Bev: I told you, /they're always watching.

Stacey: *(As Bev.)* /they're always watching.

Bev: I knew this would happen.

Matt: This is all your fault. Why did you stay behind?

Bev: I tried... I didn't...

Lily: She's sorry.

Stacey: What did they do to us?

Bev: They used the electric shock treatment again. I told them it doesn't work, it doesn't help.

Here we stand

Tim starts giving the audience his pictures whilst mumbling.

Stacey: *(To audience.)* Have you seen enough yet? You know, they put me in here because my dad died. I was the only one there. *(All patients stand and slowly walk towards Stacey.)* Is that any way to treat someone who's grieving? Can you see these scars? Can you? *(All patients touch the scars on their faces.)*

Lily: We just went to get some new Christmas lights.

Stacey: He pulled his seatbelt across because mine didn't work. I told him I didn't need it, I wanted him to have it. A car started skidding and crashed into us.

Matt: I hit my face on the dashboard.

Stacey: And the window smashed all over me. When I looked up dad wasn't there. He wasn't in the car. *(Long pause.)* He went through the windscreen. I told him to put the seatbelt on, he'd still be here if…

Bev: It was all my fault. I've been here long enough.

Stacey: Just let me out.

> *Lights start to flicker. Sounds of car horns, cars crashing, people screaming. Seven chimes of the clock. Stacey falls to the floor.*

Stacey: Dad! Dad wake up! Dad! No get off me! Dad wake up! Why isn't he moving? Dad!

Blackout. Silence.

All: Dad!

Lights up.

Bev starts to rock back and forth clawing at her arms. Tim starts frantically rubbing his drawings off the board and ripping up his drawings, throwing them at the audience. His mumbling also becomes more frantic. Lily runs into the audience as if looking for her dad.

Bev: *(Repeats, getting increasingly angry.)* He's gone. He's gone. He's gone. Why did you leave me?

Lily: Dad? Daddy? Where are you? *(Holds an audience members leg. Repeating.)* Why hasn't he come back? Where's daddy? Do you know where he is?

Matt: *(To an audience member.)* Why are you still here? Why didn't you help him? You could have done something. /This is all your fault. He would still be here if it weren't for you!

Stacey gets up and takes on the persona of Tim. She starts frantically whispering, taking drawings off the audience, ripping them up and throwing them. Tim disappears in the shadows.

Stacey: *(Takes on the persona of Lily, she holds audience members leg. Upset.)* /Why hasn't he come back? Where's daddy? Do you know where he is? *(Lily fades into the shadows.)* He should have come back. Why didn't he come back? I want him back. I want daddy back *(Takes on the persona of Bev.)* He's gone. He's gone. *He's gone.* Why did you leave me? *(Bev fades into the shadows.)* You were the only one who understood me. There's no point of being here now. *(She looks as if she is holding something to her throat.)* I want to be with you. No one will miss me. I'm coming dad. I'm coming. *(Takes on the persona of Matt.)* This is all your fault. He would still be here if it weren't for you *(Matt begins to rip Stacey's sleeves revealing cuts on her arms, which are identical to Bev's. He takes the material from her neck revealing strangulation marks similar to Bev and Lily's. Matt then slowly fades into the shadows.)* You could have helped him! Why didn't you?! WHY DIDN'T YOU?! *(She then sits on the seat on stage and turns back into Stacey).* I'm not meant to be here.

Blackout.

ROSS HORTON is a student from Oldbury. He enjoys writing whenever he is not listening to music, at work, or asleep. His influences include Rimbaud, Jim Morrison, Buddhist Sutras, Rilke, Baudelaire, Kenneth Anger, Lautreamont and Roman Polanski. His favourite poetic work is Rimbaud's *Illuminations* and his favourite novel is *Lolita*.

Untitled
by Ross Horton

Humanity has shed its scaled skin -
opened its eye to the ferrous dawn that awaited us in the
   golden night
It is not afraid of the Ghosts of hidden gardens,
   the crocodiles in the valleys of clover.

The azure pool spirits us on and draws us away from sin.
   Enclosed within the concrete sea are the drained sharks of
   minutes lost to fields abroad. The little brown book of idiocy
   lies naked and raped on the side of the frosty highway.

Enlightenment is yours, if you want to
White faces count your life away and rescind the hope of our
   last rushed pact.
Witches in little yellow coats steam our regal windows but
   cannot get in.

Smooth hypocrisy lies dormant in us, but cannot release itself -
   it has time yet to serve
A piano screams in the north-west corner of the room waiting
   to be euthanized
Wailing concepts engulf our lost splendid poetry
Death to flaccid war!

FRANCISCO IANNUZZI has been writing ever since he learned to write. His work has been widely unpublished, notably a series of seven comics called *Paco-man* after his own nickname. Since that golden age he has written countless emails, text messages, status updates and tweets but this is his first published story.

He is bilingual in English and Spanish but his writing in the latter is very basic. He's no Sabato, he says, but he hopes that this will improve with time along with his work in English.

Mi Viejo
by Francisco Iannuzzi

I'm standing in the kitchen barefoot and slightly stoned as I wait for the kettle to boil. Dad is talking and gesturing in his Italian way, one that has been passed down through generations dating back to the old country, *il paese*. He's crossing his arms and then uncrossing them, I can tell he feels a draught coming from the dining room door that's been left open. He keeps hugging and un-hugging himself because he's cold. I'm looking down at myself mirroring his stance, his stoop and I'm even starting to feel the draught on my feet. He says, "Put some socks on, you'll get a cold." Twenty-two years old and I still get the same shit. Like the, "put a coat on!" just before I go out; it will never be any different. Today though I don't mind. He's talking me through the scenes before and after his colonoscopy, signaling the moment with his coarse and over-sized index finger. I'm considering that the thickness of his finger must have been determined by the size of his nose. I'm staring at his big pointer and imagining it going into his deep nostrils. It makes sense - you'd need a digit that size to pick such a honk. He's laughing at the whole procedure, from the anaesthesia to the vision he had half way through, while the camera was up there, being poked around. He thought he'd dreamt the nurse telling him, "Luis, can you see the screen there, that's what was seen on your scan. It's nothing Luis, nothing more to worry about." This as it turned out was not a dream at all.

The colonoscopy was all because of a blotch found on a scan doctors had performed on him a few months prior. He'd had some severe back pain that was as a result of some kidney stones. Considering his age they said it was better to be safe and check it out. The whole thing was a big deal for Dad. Generally we men struggle with medical tests in which the results could be either: it's nothing, or it's cancer, one of the worst cancers there is and by the way it's up your arse. It took long enough for Mum to convince him that a prostate check made good sense. This, for Louie, was a huge step. But he was scared, naturally. He was born in Argentina and raised by Italians so fear was a natural part of growing up for him. This was not going to change now at 56.

When I've talked with Dad about his childhood he manages to recall some very early memories. This, as you'll come to see, is probably a result of what some would say he had experienced (I would say he had endured). He remembers at the age of 3 his mother (or Nona as she is called by her grandchildren) putting him on a stool and saying to him with a pointed finger, "Luisito, Mama needs to go and run some errands. If you move from this stool, you'll die." and there he sat obediently, waiting for her to return, not moving from the stool. The ways of the old seem alien to us, although I could say that sometimes they seem more effective. Nona had very little help whilst Nono (grandfather) was at work. She could not take my Dad everywhere with her so she would have to do some things alone and find ways of coping. Inevitably such occasions and moments are reflected in his personality today, and as I watch him I can feel them around... affecting and even changing me... At an early age Nona set in the place the foundations of his need for her. She did this with a combination of cleverly worded stories and great food, which of course amplified the hold that all mothers have on their children. Religion and witchcraft were other forms of conditioning used. She often suggested, and still does, that she can cure headaches, stomach pains and liver pains with a tape measure and a prayer. In a *Green Mile* kind of way she performs this ritual and proceeds to 'yawn out' the bad stuff - although you can't actually see the bad stuff, it just looks like she is yawning. It's weird.

What's weirder is that it works. She used these things to have him at her mercy.

Unavoidably he contracted some of the famous *Nona-isms* that we, in the family, all know and have come to love; one being his superstitious and cockeyed sensibility. His fear of snakes comes directly from her attempts at getting him to sleep in his own bed when he was a child. After another night of running in and wriggling himself in-between my Grandparents Nona told him, "turn over the pillow so you get the cold side." Little did Luisito know that she had placed a piece of brown lace underneath it, so that as he turned it over she could start screaming, "SNAKE! SNAKE! LUISITO RUN!" Luisito would never try to sleep in Nona and Nono's bed again. *A Mental Scarring Effect* best describes this type of parenting.

The eldest of three, Dad is a walking representation of what the Italian immigrants of Argentina are known for. It's engraved in his flesh, in the dark remnants of oil left in the cracks of his skin. They're far from dirty, instead full of graft and history. Hardened from having to help build the house that my Grandparents still live in today, from the shoes he had to sew in the downstairs cobbler's that my Grandparents ran as a second job (aside from Nono's daily labouring) and from the tools he has handled since he was 11 years of age. A toolmaker by trade, working class by inheritance.

It's 1963 and Calle Pueyrredon in Virreyes, Buenos Aires is just a dusty street with very few houses on it. The *Pan Americana* football pitches are visible from the corner where the house is; situated on the left and right hand side of the *Pan American Highway*, which runs from Ushuaia, Argentina (the furthest point south in the country) up to Prudhoe Bay, Alaska. The highway is about 100 yards away from the front door, which is slowly opening. An 8-year-old Luisito peaks out with his head first, then steps out rubbing his eyes free from their sleep. He steps out bare foot and starts to walk towards the next house along, which is across the road and to the right for about 50 meters. The road is hot but his soles are thick and hard from hours spent kicking that ball around. He awoke to an empty house, no Nona and no word of where she was. Confused, he drags himself towards the place he hopes may show some sign of life; sporting just his favoured white Y fronts and nothing else. He knocks, and when they answer he asks if they've seen her.

My Auntie Liliana, who is two years younger than him, told me a story of an occasion when she and my father were fighting. She did not remember exactly what about, but she remembers that she was aged around five or six. On hearing the ruckus Nona came out of the kitchen and into the dining area, prepped for battle. (Preferred forms of punishment would be slapping or hitting with whatever was in hand at the time: cane, broom, spoon even slipper.) After Luis received his lashing on the back of the legs, Nona moved swiftly towards Lili. She struggled and moved out of the way. She *ran* out of the way, and as *La Gorda* caught up with her, grabbed her, and drew back to give this flogging a bit of extra kick, Luisito managed to get between her hand and his sister. "Don't hit her Ma! Don't! Run Lili! Run!" She ran; and Luisito got seconds.

I guess if we are to attribute to Nona certain negative, or rather *distinctive* character traits found in Dad, maybe we should acknowledge his bravery as being something she instilled in him also. But I don't think it was. This was all him. It's who is in front of me talking about his colonoscopy, with a grateful smile, at midnight on a Thursday, as he waits up for his eldest son to return home from work, so that he can move his car and leave him a parking spot outside the front of the house.

The story as to how my mother (Cecilia) and my father got married has been brought into question many times, with Dad often changing certain things on retelling it. But this is as it was the last time I asked him.

The year was 1977 and Luis said to Cecilia; "If next year Argentina win the world cup, I'll marry you." Well, they only went and won it! When she happened to bring this up in conversation with him after the tournament, he vanished for a week and then came back and said; "yeah ok we probably should get married." (I definitely inherited my mother's ideals of romance.)

After getting married, Luis and Cecilia worked and began saving money. They planned on buying some land and building a house. In Argentina the tradition, even today, is that you buy a plot of land and that you build your own home, to your own tastes. This can be both a good or bad thing. Houses are often built up in a strange variety of architectural styles; some look stable, some definitely don't and some don't even look finished. Luis asked his parents and his parents-in-law for money. Both turned him away, one said; "well, yeah I was kind of saving that money...I know you'll pay it back but I can't..." and the other said; "Luis, no. I have no money for you." (I'm hoping by now you can guess which one of my Grandmothers gave the second response). Mum and Dad knew then that they had no option but to live with Nona whilst they saved, which would have taken a while since Mum wasn't working full-time and she was still studying. Instead, Luis decided to find another way of funding the construction of his own home. With so many family members in Italy - which he and my mother had visited on their honeymoon – he arranged for some work out there and went to earn some money to bring back.

After four or five months in Milan, with Tio Giuseppe, the distance - along with the lengthy exchange of letters between him and Cecilia - eroded his patience and his *alma*, so he returned. The money he had was just enough to buy a plot of land and make a start at least. In the mean time he and my mother rented the downstairs apartment under Nona and

Nono's house; a one bedroom, one toilet, one kitchen and one table and chairs kind of vibe.

1983 Cecilia shot out sprog *numero uno*, Juan Luis Iannuzzi a.k.a my big brother. Around this time Mum was working as a psychiatric doctor and the family where still in the downstairs apartment. Dad had brought the plot of land and had already started digging the foundations. 1986 Argentina won the world cup, again, thanks to Diego Armando Maradona (what a guy). The same year Cecilia had baby number two, but after some complications, due to a premature birth, the child died only a week after being born. In July Mum buys a bunch of lilies and puts them in the same vase that sits by the living room window; and that's pretty much my only connection to what would have been my other big brother. 1988 Cecilia was pregnant again, this time with me - but don't worry I make it through.

The development of what was to be our home had stopped and started around the arrivals of the children Cecilia was having (and probably all the various fun times she and Luis spent making them too). After my birth things moved quickly.

Cecilia and Luis saw an opportunity to emigrate to England. Family was in place with some immediate work so, the call was made to pack up and leave. I was born and within days Luis was on a plane flying over to Northampton, to set things in place for the arrival of the rest of the clan. At the airport the whole family came out to say goodbye to Dad. My brother was inconsolable, my mother had me in her arms, Nono's tears were falling from behind his gold-framed bifocals and Nona stood by him, crying too. As Dad - no longer Luisito - stood in front of his mother, he put his left hand on her right shoulder and before moving in close for a kiss goodbye pointed at her - just like the Nona that had him on a stool, putting the fear of death in him - and said; "don't cry now, don't cry. Because when I came to you and asked you for help, you turned me away." He couldn't help it. He had to say something; he had to let her know she'd hurt him. Realizing that he had to then board a plane and fly for thirteen hours he kissed her, hugged her hard and said; "I love you."

The plane landed at London Heathrow. He wasn't looking for Nona anymore; he was leaving her behind. He was putting it all on the line for Cecilia, Juan and Francisco and because of that here we are. My brother, now a commercial pilot for *Ryanair* and me: musician, writer and above all grateful. Above all else, privileged... But Nona is still there and we want her to be because of course we love her. She is, despite her eccentric form of parenting, an incredible Grandmother. But for Luisito, Luis, Louie, Dad, she was the opposition. I guess Nona was the symbol of things he couldn't have, be it her help, her affection, even after his sacrifices. Having to work at the age of 9 and 10 sewing shoes so that the whole family could get by, instead of being outside, playing football, following the dream that so many young boys have in Argentina of one day making it. Not having the support to do that, support which he now gives to my brother and me, unwaveringly. Having to help his parents build their home and have her refuse to help him build his, he had to be away from her, he had to take *us* away from her, maybe... to hurt her...

Juan is back from work. Dad hears the car outside without even looking; the sound of his slippers on the wooden laminate flooring is quick, as he makes straight for the front door. The colonoscopy talk has been cut short; I put a hint of Ballentine's in and finish making my cup of tea. I'm heading up to my room but for some reason can't get it all out of my head – probably the weed I've been inhaling all night. I've spilt some tea on my desk... and where's that sock? Perhaps I should write all this down.

BRUCE JOHNS is a lapsed academic, kept man and writer of prose who pounds the keyboard during the day and then incinerates dinner. This story represents his fifth appearance in the Anthology and his second collaboration as editor, a record fatal to the idea that practice makes perfect. More evidence of his failings can be found on his website at www.brucejohns.co.uk.

Signore Bigshot
by Bruce Johns

"*Mano su mano.*"

Guido placed over his companion's hand, with its writer's callus and childlike absence of rings, his own plump and predatory paw. He noticed, as if with her eyes, a pouch of flesh at the base of his thumb, the liver spots which made his skin look unclean. He was like this about his physical self, never morbid or excessively vain but alive to its humours and flaws: the billowing from muscle to flab which started years ago, the subtle encroachments of age.

This was a trademark routine, a verbal prank that could turn its hand to seduction or philosophy. The first couplet was an excuse to make contact, a small liberty gauging the level of response. After that, of course, the words were on their own.

He closed his hand around hers and said "*Mano in mano*", the middle word stressed to indicate a natural progression. She stiffened momentarily, more in surprise than alarm, her eyes fixed on his mouth like someone who senses a trick is being performed and wants to know how. Was he running ahead of himself? They had known each other less than an hour yet something about her had made him impetuous, an unfamiliar braiding of sharpness and naivety. For once it was not clear what outcome he desired.

His grip relaxed and she moved her hand out of range under the guise of shaking her glass to see if the ice, which was all that remained of her drink, had melted.

He pressed on.

"*Mano su cosa*".

This came with a shrug, readable as indifference or apology. From her lack of response it seemed that no offence had been taken. She was strikingly plain, with hair cut boyishly for convenience rather than effect, no make-up of any kind and blunt, unpainted nails. He was used to women who powdered, varnished and tinted themselves, the whole chemistry set applied with brushes and pads, pencils with soft, inky noses and little cushions that, dabbed onto cheek or chin, released a flattering pollen. Was it her lack of disguise that intrigued him, with its suggestion of candour? In love, as in business, no one came at you straight.

"Mano in cosa."

A note of regret now entered his voice as if discovering, in this most intimate of topics, a sadness hitherto undetected. He reached across the table, so that his cufflinks emerged from the sleeves of his jacket and slid towards her like a bribe. His hands opened upwards, seeking permission to continue.

"No need," she said, coming to as if from a trance. "I think I can see where this is heading. *Cosa su cosa?*"

The pronunciation was a travesty. Still, a note in her voice encouraged him, wary yet not regretful, pleased to have spotted what was coming but lured by this conceit into a kind of complicity. He was used to a battle of wits with women, in business when the occasion arose, but usually with lovers and wives exacting a price for their dependence. In both cases he mostly prevailed, took the odd reverse with good grace, but never felt diminished in what he thought of as the masculine territory of the mind. This American was different. It was not usual for him to be so clumsily upstaged, with no feeling for the protocols of flirtation.

He nodded, inclining his head in recognition of her astuteness. She laughed, a little too triumphantly, so that the case for bedding her was strengthened by the prospect of revenge, and drained the melted water from the bottom of her glass.

"Another?" he asked and, without looking round, raised his left hand. A waiter appeared at once through the muddle of occupied tables and Guido asked for a Diet Coke. The man retreated backwards for the first few steps as if leaving royalty.

"Wow," she said, "the habit of command. That was impressive."

"One of the few advantages of age," he corrected her sorrowfully.

She laughed again and wagged a finger at him, standing up and looping the strap of her bag over one shoulder. "You won't make me feel sorry for you. And when I come back I wanna hear your story. I've spilled the beans, so it's only fair."

She set off through the labyrinth of parasols with the swagger of a woman not used to male attention, passing into and out of the shade so that she seemed to flicker on and off. Then, reaching an impasse created by two large tables she was forced to double back, pointedly not looking his way. It was a reverse that aroused his sympathy, not often a bedfellow of desire.

He reflected on what she had said. 'Spilled the beans' was new to him, although its meaning was clear. She had told him a lot, that American compulsion to bare their souls, and the rest was easy to read. Her first name was Helen, her second Polish-sounding, like a mouthful of pins. She was in her early 30s, a teacher at some university he had never heard of. And single, her experience of men confined to bookish types, their lovemaking awkward, no doubt, the pillow talk competitive. As for being in Padova, the frescoes had something to do with it, a greater if drier passion for research.

But there remained a mystery about her interest in him. American women looking for a holiday romance were commonplace, at least in films, but gondoliers and ski-instructors were the stuff of such fantasies. He was old enough to be a father figure, another cliché with some basis in fact, but she was surely too smart for that.

Yet she did seem drawn to him, and the fact that he couldn't tell why made their meeting feel almost providential. It had happened at the Post Office. Helen was waiting to buy stamps for some postcards. She was in the wrong queue, which she might have realised given that everyone around her was carrying parcels. He pointed out her mistake in his rather courtly English, then, observing that the correct queue would take even longer, offered to intercede when her turn came. The man at the counter, sensing a class enemy, at first declined to help, with a note of regret that was angled away from him to discourage any appeal. Guido brought out the worst in union men, to the point where his staff kept him away from negotiations, at least until it was time for the fountain pen and the photographs. But he played up the lady's innocence and the length of the other queue and located a gloating chivalry in his compatriot that finally won the day.

"Thank you so much," she gushed, as they left the building together. "I think I would have been there forever."

He shook his head. "Italian men can never resist a beautiful woman. It is I who should be grateful. With a coffee maybe?"

Rather than accepting his flattery as a step in a dance, the opening move in a game barely started, she seemed genuinely affected and confused, as if this kind of offer was new to her. Which, looking at her clothes, might have been the case.

"That would be nice. But something cold, perhaps. This heat is unbearable."

Which was how, an hour later, he came to be waiting for her return, still trying to get a fix on what had passed between them and wondering which of his own beans to spill. He was, self-evidently, a businessman and it was probably safe to disclose that he manufactured glass. The factory visible from local trains was a landmark that usually impressed. She might also like to know that his grandfather, a leading figure in employers' organisations, had needed protection from the Red Brigades. Danger, like money, was an aphrodisiac, and unlike money worked better at one remove. But should he reveal that the old man's driver packed a gun? The sight of its harness, as his jacket fell open, was to young Guido as exciting a peek into the adult world as a strap glimpsed below a woman's dress – a form of titillation lost on the young of today, whose underwear seemed to be worn on top of their clothes.

His personal circumstances might be harder to sell. He was not only married but a serial collector and loser of wives. Lucia, the latest Signora Carlotti, was at the house near Asolo, where he joined her at weekends. At that precise moment, it being useful to know her whereabouts, she was having a manicure, a scene he knew well, Lucia holding forth on the latest gossip while the girl, dressed like a dental nurse, bowed over her hand as if pledging allegiance. Their distance apart looked like estrangement, when really it was only logistics, the need for him to be close to the plant. But the apartment she knew about in Padova was only one of two he owned, the other on the company's books and occupied by his mistress. This complication would be even less politic to reveal, although as it happened Federica was away, visiting her mother. That is why he had been at the post office, sending her birthday present. "*Cara Fred*," went the inscription inside, the diminutive, like their affection, depleted and ironic.

All that was the easy part, however, matters he could disclose or not in response to signals received. What lay beneath was more delicate and personal, one's secret history that, if unwisely disclosed, incurred the ultimate disadvantage in any negotiation: that of being understood. For Guido the turning point, the moment when his view of the world was forged, had come at the age of fourteen. He attended a boarding school run by the Church, an Order his family was close to, financially and through relatives taking vows, a tithe of four-eyed cousins and unmarriageable aunts. His grades were promising but his chief passion was sport. He boxed, swam, rowed but above all ran, 400 metres his distance, in the top three nationally for his age. His prowess and physique were pagan virtues, pandered to by the school in the interests of publicity and morale. And when he became ill for the first time in his life, a fever that kept him in bed for several days, his body astonished him with a new range of powers: the veering between heat and cold, wild imaginings, a debility he came to enjoy. The job of nursing him fell to the nuns who, far from displaying any vocation for their role, seemed to delight in having the weakness of the flesh confirmed. Except that one night he woke to find a younger woman in attendance, the colour of her habit merging with the dark, the bright square of her face floating disembodied about the room. Coming close she stroked his forehead and asked how he was. The touch of her hand startled him, after days of convent-style asperity.

His dry lips parted reluctantly. "*Meglio, grazie,*" he said, the whisper, all he could manage, creating an air of conspiracy. She sat next to him and continued to stroke his forehead, the sheets stretched tight by her weight on the bed. Modesty and propriety, those twin spoilsports of the soul, had not yet stirred from his sleep and he was filled with a delicious, dream-like sense of possibility.

Her lips moved again. He had suffered, they said, but was now to be redeemed. She called him Christ's brother and her breath so close to his ear made the Virgin's love sound intimate and physical, each small projectile of air a luscious blasphemy. Leaning forward she rearranged the covers. His pyjama jacket, standard issue despite his temperature, hung open and her sleeve trailed across his chest . In the far distance he could feel something stiffen and unfurl.

The look they exchanged had, in a way, lasted all his life. There was no need for words; he had only to touch her hand. But the enormity of what he was thinking got the better of him. She was the embodiment of chastity, the ultimate taboo. The wrath of God converged in his imagination with the outrage of the school and his father's fury, a trinity of male tempers it would be useless, and terrible, to oppose.

He did nothing. The moment passed. Within days, fully recovered, he wasn't sure if it had happened at all. But a mythical kind of significance attached itself to the memory, which grew more vivid and frustrating with time. His Temptation, he called it, a bible story with the moral reversed: religion a pantomime, self-denial a lie. The nun's breath in his ear became a gale that flattened the case for obedience. He slackened off on his studies. Hung up his oars and his gloves. Even stopped running – except, figuratively-speaking, after girls. By the time he left school and joined the family firm he had made up his mind: that one failure of nerve was the last regret he would allow himself. From then on he would live by his own rules, and no one else's.

And so it had been, although the headlong rush after profit and pleasure had tempered over the years. Proportion, a classical virtue, was his watchword now. Nor was he quite so hard on the Church these days. As in tennis, the sport of middle age, he needed an opponent worthy of his game. The reformers whose cause he had been known to fund (a small magazine, that symposium on celibacy) deluded themselves. Sooner or later chipping away at the old certainties would bring the whole edifice crashing down. In this respect, at least, his old Jesuit teachers were right: truth had to be hard in order to be clear. Like glass.

"Guido?"

The sound of his name startled him. It was Helen, returned from the bathroom.

"You were miles away."

"Yes. A business matter. But now we have both returned. I was thinking," a lie, it had only just entered his head, "do you want to see the frescoes again? I would like to hear you talk about them."

"Are you sure? You aren't busy? The truth, now."

"Of course."

"But we'll never get in. You have to book days in advance."

"Please. This is something I can do."

"Say, you really do pull strings around here. Okay. But don't think you're off the hook. You can tell me all about yourself on the way."

The waiter appeared bearing on a small tray a tall glass chunky with ice that chimed as he set it down.

"Do you mind?" Helen asked. "I'm gasping."

The bill paid, the waiter left, side-stepping tables without slowing down, one of those lower order skills one could admire without envy. Guido watched Helen swallow the drink in a series of long, masculine gulps. She really had no idea. And at that moment he experienced a feeling of transcendent joy as everything – his hard-earned knowledge of the world, this woman who proved that surprise was still possible, even the people laughing at other tables – became, like planets, propitiously aligned.

"Okay," she said, setting the glass down. "I'm done. Is it far from here? I mean, it's too hot to walk." They set off down a side street and she carried on in short, nervous sentences. "Will you get a cab? I bet one appears the moment you step onto the sidewalk. Signore Bigshot. You give directions but I'm gonna pay. "

***

She went into the Chapel ahead of him, while he stayed in the anteroom trying to persuade the attendant to give her more time. He refused, resentful of the phone call he had received allowing them to jump the queue. Guido could feel it again, the hackles rising on a union man.

Inside he found her gazing up at the walls, head thrown back and mouth slightly parted.

"There are limits to my influence, it seems. Ten minutes and no more. The man here is very... official."

She spoke without looking away.

"That's fine, the frescos come first. And I have been here before. But thank you for trying."

His failure still rankled.

"Two people for a few extra minutes, what does he think will happen? Or one, I can wait outside."

She didn't seem to be listening, and he took advantage of the moment to look at her in profile, the curves of her face flattened as she offered it up to the wall, the body unaware of itself inside the functional clothes. In the taxi the problem of bean-spilling had been solved by talking about his endowment of the university. How easily she had been deflected by professional interest. He tried to imagine her in bed: all arms and legs, probably, like someone learning to swim.

"You sweat a little,' he went on, 'and molecules of salt attack the paint. Or your heat increases the temperature by the smallest part of a degree and something beautiful is lost. It is the same between people. We always damage what we love."

"Guido, are you a philosopher?"

He pulled another of his faces. "No, just a practical man."

She laughed too loud, and with too much familiarity, a complete innocent or clumsily overplaying her hand. His feelings towards her had advanced and retreated more than once and were now on the turn again. Oddly for a lover of women picking up strangers was not his style, and he should really be at work. His secretary had called while they were in the taxi and his lie, so like deceiving a wife, seemed to have encouraged Helen, sitting by his side.

"Which picture interests you?" he asked, making conversation.

"Here," she said, "the Resurrection of Lazarus. See how out of scale the labourers are, moving the stone. Like children really. I guess he just ran out of room so made them small. But that's my point. The working man was expendable."

"And that is what your book is about?"

"Article, yes. Compare this with a Breughel, say, The Census at Bethlehem, where the common folk steal the show. The place of ordinary people changes over time till we get to Courbet's stonebreakers taking centre stage. At that point we've moved away from the labour of religion and on to the religion of labour. Or that's what I'm trying to show...'

For a while she had sounded rapt in her subject, and totally convinced, in that way experts had of talking to themselves. Then, remembering she had an audience, her voice trailed off as if unsure of itself.

"We live in less religious times," he said, helpfully.

"Well yes," she agreed, eager and earnest once more, "but what's interesting is that the notion of sacredness itself remains. We just attach it to different things."

He felt unqualified to judge her knowledge of art, although occasions like this brought out the patriot in him, a feeling for beauty part of the national conceit.

"And you prefer the paintings where the ordinary people are more important?"

"My own taste is beside the point. I don't criticise Giotto for these little men, although it's kind of obvious to me what he's done."

"The proletariat of the miracle," he said, thinking aloud.

"Hey," she exclaimed, "that's good. Can I use it?"

He acted powerless to refuse and went on. "I wonder if they were organised."

"Who?"

"Giotto's little men, as you call them. What union did they belong to?"

"The Guild of Stone Rollers, I guess."

His laugh started out as polite but then found a more genuine second wind. She had passed the test of having a sense of humour about her work. More, she had dropped her guard, something unthinkable to the women he knew, and entered into his clumsy attempt to make fun of ideas that mattered to her. Whatever this amounted to, inexperience perhaps or generosity, the pendulum of his interest, so erratic over the last two hours, had swung back in her direction. There was a tempo, a rhythm to these things and the moment had come to choose.

He glanced at his watch.

"Our ten minutes are almost finished, I am afraid. We should leave, before our friend in the office has us arrested."

Instead of following him she turned towards the altar end of the chapel, sank easily to one knee and crossed herself. Of course, he thought, the Polish name. Instinctively he looked away.

They congregated, the two of them, in the heat outside. This phase of their encounter had run its course. Under normal circumstances whatever reason they found for prolonging it would only be a pretext, but she seemed so unaware of the rules that any suggestion he made might be taken literally.

"Are you hungry?" he asked.

"Ravenous," she said. Her face translated the word, which was new to him.

"I have very little in my kitchen. Some spaghetti, perhaps, *con aglio e olio*?"

"I don't want to put you to any trouble."

"It is nothing. A little of this," he mimed a chopping motion, "and this," he did the same with shaking a pan, "and then a few minutes of this," leaning forward to an imaginary fork.

"You have lots of little routines, don't you? I bet you use them on all the girls. Which reminds me, we never finished the one from the café."

"But I thought you knew the last line."

"Let me see." She put a forefinger under her chin and pretended to think. "How about *cosa in cosa*?"

"Yes," he said, gravely, so that the levity bled from her face. "That is usually how it ends."

They took another taxi to the apartment. She went to the bathroom which gave him a chance to hide the photograph of Lucia in a drawer. As expected, he was obliged to cook lunch. She watched the garlic being sliced and called him an artist, then wandered round the apartment while the water boiled and the pasta was tossed in oil. When it was ready he found her inspecting a piece of glass. She seemed calm enough but the vase was shaking.

"Not one of your company's," she said gracelessly. It occurred to him that these blunders accounted for the erotic friction. Perhaps an element of dislike was necessary for desire, or you were left with friendship and how did that work with a woman? The vase needed rescuing, and in laying hold of it he touched her briefly. Hand on hand.

As with so much about Helen, who had been wrong-footing him all day, his expectations of her in bed were well wide of the mark. She lay still and tense, like someone frightened of bees. The whole thing was a mistake but he kept going out of courtesy and then impatience, with her or himself it hardly mattered.

Afterwards, to his consternation, there was blood. She was the resourceful one now, as if this had been the whole point of the exercise. She went to the bathroom where taps could be heard, and splashing, then returned with a towel soaked in water with which, kneeling, she attended to the bed.

"Helen, no, please, it does not matter," he said, but to no effect. She placed one hand under the sheet in order to wash it from the top, and her fingers – even, faintly, the colour of her skin – showed through the wet cotton. The Shroud came to mind, or something else connected with death. How doggedly religion pursued him, like a lawyer claiming copyright on someone else's design. He shivered and put on a robe but she was oblivious to her nakedness which seemed, in the air of crisis that had taken over, a minor indignity.

"I did not know..." he began, but without looking away from the bed she held up a hand, decisively, like a traffic policeman.

"I don't want to talk about it, okay? There's no reason for you to feel... I probably owe you an apology. I had my own agenda. But it's fine, really. I'll just finish up here and..."

She got to her feet and turned away from him at the same time. He watched her leave the room, clothes in a bundle along with the towel. After making love he was used to viewing a woman differently, his body having lost interest, the recovery period longer these days. But so much about Helen spoke of awkwardness and vulnerability that had become more affecting, not less, of disadvantage in a market so clearly rigged in favour of the well-appointed.

She emerged fully dressed, stuffing the towel into her bag.

"I'll send you a new one. No, I insist. And please don't think badly of me. You're a sweet guy, just what I was looking for. I knew I'd be in safe hands."

One benefit of not wearing make-up, he realised, is that nothing smudges or runs when you cry. Her tears overspilled onto a blank canvas, and her hand was clean when she wiped them away.

"Helen, I am the one who must apologise. The first time should be more...meaningful."

She laughed, tripping over a catch in her voice.

"Your English is wonderful, Guido, did I tell you? No one uses words like that anymore, at least about this." She indicated the bed with its damp, exhausted sheets. "And don't worry, it had plenty of meaning, for me at least."

She held out her hand for him to shake. It was an absurd way to part, but he had nothing better to propose. That being all he was allowed to hold, he raised the hand to his lips. The taste, complicated by soap but otherwise quite natural, was not unlike his own when, as a boy, he had used his arm to practise kissing, a memory that returned to him now from some unsealed vault, along with the dull, post-operative ache of the past.

"A gentleman to the end," she said. "Goodbye, Guido. And please don't feel bad. This is what I wanted."

He showed her out and went into the kitchen, where the plates of spaghetti had gone cold. After sprinkling a little parmesan over one he forked some of the pasta into his mouth and began eating mechanically, his mind on other things. The whole episode had been so devoid of the usual refinements that he felt ashamed, although it turned out he was the one who had been used. Phoning his secretary helped: a Canadian double glazing company was in town and the arrangements needed to be confirmed. Mid-western winters, Helen had said when explaining where she lived: a true test of glass. He took a shower before leaving for the office. Glancing down he noticed some of her blood on him, already dry. It looked ancient, somehow, like paint on a chapel wall.

It was not until morning that he discovered her room key half under the bed. It must have fallen from her bag or from a pocket as she undressed, shyly turning away from him. He rang the hotel. The receptionist had not been on duty the day before but knew who he meant. She had just checked out and left for the station. This information registered somehow, but Guido had stopped listening after the first few words. He had heard her called Sister, and there was a buzzing noise in his ears.

He lived not far from the station and set off on foot, with no idea what to say if he arrived in time. Nuns in plain clothes, tearing up their vows: word of such liberties had reached him but nothing on this scale. It felt like a trick played by fate, a joke of cosmic proportions. To bring everything down about one's head was the real measure of holding nothing sacred, a test he had failed once before. Now, for a second time, that transgression had been denied. By the act itself, so maladroit. By the irony of not knowing. And most of all by another intruder on his fulfilment, a sorrow whose origin he could not quite place. Of course, a shadow of sadness attended any satisfaction, but this felt different. More particular. More profound.

He began to quicken, not the ponderous sprint of the tennis court but in hopeful imitation of a younger self. His muscles were out of practice, his lungs felt shallow and unused, but he forced his legs to move faster, pumping those arms as he had been taught, as if jabbing an assailant trying to grab him from behind. This portly caricature of an athlete was what bystanders commented on afterwards, and the way he fell, with hands outstretched, as runners sometimes do when they are desperate for the line.

DEREK LITTLEWOOD teaches literature in The School of English, Birmingham City University. He attended an Arvon writing course taught by David Morley and Alison MacLeod on which the first draft of *Night Fishing* was caught. Subsequently he has written poetry more intensively and has benefitted from workshops at the Poetry School. He is drawn by the dark side of the landscape, the birth and death of silver photography and the texture of language.

Night Fishing
by Derek Littlewood

When it happened, Sam felt a tenderness, an itching as if his shoulders had been in too much sun. Lifting his shirt with exploring fingers, instead of flakes of sunburned skin, he felt the faintest touch of down, then stubble like an unshaved jaw. A hint of goose quills like the wing his mother kept from Michaelmas to sweep the pastry board. Hauling up his shirt, he tried to look behind at his own back, but unsuccessfully. He might as well try to see the back of his own head without a mirror. It was as well his mate was sorting the dregs of the catch, turned away from the skipper. They had needed to go much further out to sea these days as the herring fishery was drying up inshore. Some said that soon there would be no more herring to be had. Sam turned the bows into the waves, hauling the main sheet in to trim the sail. They were sailing close to the wind. They must be mad or desperate to fish with the night coming on so far from home. Near the banks they dropped their nets and suddenly began to catch the herring. A feast of herring. The boat settled in the water with the weight of the catch. Almost imperceptibly a storm was coming on. Dark rain hissing over the surface of the sea. The boat began to pitch. Used to poor weather, he gritted his teeth determinedly and pulled down his sou'wester. There was a change in the sea, the boat began to pitch and roll violently. Sam fought to keep her head to wind. Heavy weather was coming aboard now. Sam shouted a warning to his mate, as they were lifted and smashed sideways on to the waves with water coming over the gunwales. There was salt everywhere in his mouth, in his eyes and down his nose. His shoulders were burning; despite the storm he wrenched off his oilskin coat, his back naked to the elements. There was the faintest stink of sulphur. Balanced over the side of the boat now, he began to haul desperately at the nets, heaving with silvery fish. Should he cut the nets free with his claspknife to lose the weight of the catch which threatened to overturn them? They began to ship a lot of water, the sea flooding in torrents now over the side. Water was up to his waist, salt and cold, inside his boots and oil skin trousers. As they capsized and he felt the hull slip away from him, Sam felt the pull of something outside of himself, a noise like the rushing of vast wings. He felt immense calm, a stillness came over the sea. Amazingly his mate was singing at the top of his voice just as they did each Sunday in chapel. Then Sam seemed to drift above the boat, looking down upon it as one might view a toy floating adrift in the village pond from the top of an oak tree.

KATE MASCARENHAS is a PhD student of children's literature. She writes articles on British comics, animation, and science fiction. Currently she is also juggling drafts of two fantasy novels. *The Riparian* is an extract from her first feature length screenplay.

The Riparian
by Kate Mascarenhas

                                          FADE IN:

EXT. COURTYARD. DAY

Crumbling brick walls. White tin cans heaped on the concrete. A dead place; nothing grows here.

Amongst the cans is a human arm.

Severed at the elbow.

Blistered.

The fingertips scorched.

INT. LAB/BASEMENT. DAY

Cramped, strewn with paper. A ten foot machine hums. It has a screen. A digital clock. A speaker with a microphone. Dials.

And most important: a black hole the size of a human head. The hole is haloed with blue neon light.

                    SPEAKER
          Cairns?

CAIRNS sits at a table, right arm always beneath the surface. She is sixtyish. Her face is stoic, and suggests a soldier more than a scientist. She reads a newspaper.

                    SPEAKER
          Cairns?

A MOUSE races over the page. The headline: Three Million Killed by Vesicant Bomb.

CAIRNS watches the MOUSE scamper to the floor. It scales the wall...and runs into the hole.

CAIRNS flinches.

EXT. COURTYARD. DAY

The mouse materialises in mid-air.

Twists as it falls.

It's dead by the time it hits the canisters.

The fur charrs.

INT. CORRIDOR. DAY

Fluorescent light.

No windows. HALDINE, a man who thinks very highly of himself, leads MARVELL past a line of closed doors. She is a young, smiley woman with "new girl" written all over her.

> HALDINE
> Don't worry about the maze. You'll mostly be in the lab.

INT. LAB/BASEMENT. DAY

CAIRNS is still staring at the hole when HALDINE ushers MARVELL into the room.

> HALDINE
> Marvell, this is Cairns. Cairns, Marvell. She is going to be helping us dispatch test canisters.

He turns his attention to the display screen. MARVELL offers CAIRNS her hand.

> MARVELL
> Pleased to meet you.

CAIRNS smiles, nods, and returns to her newspaper. MARVELL is disconcerted. She puts her hand in her pocket.

> SPEAKER
> Cairns?

HALDINE presses the button next to the microphone.

> HALDINE
> It's Haldine.

> SPEAKER
> Could you tell Cairns the current canister is ten minutes overdue.

> HALDINE
> (sighing)
> I'll dispatch it now.

> MARVELL
> Can I help with that?

> HALDINE
> Sure. Of course it would be great if once in a while Cairns could answer when she's spoken to.

For MARVELL's benefit, HALDINE gestures towards CAIRNS then taps his temple. CAIRNS smirks.

> HALDINE
> Unfortunately this place employs you for life. We're stuck with her until she shuffles off the mortal coil.

He opens a drawer to reveal rows of white canisters, like oversized bullets in a cartridge box. He pulls one out. It is a brighter, shinier version of the cans in the courtyard.

> HALDINE
> This is the baby. Your job's pretty simple but you've got to get it right. See this?

He runs his thumb over some iridescent numbers on the side of the canister. A digital clock - keeping time too.

> MARVELL
> Yep.

> HALDINE
> You've got to make sure that matches the clock up there to... the... nanosecond.

                    MARVELL
          OK.

                    HALDINE
          Datestamp the base and it's ready to go.
          The destination is centrally controlled
          so you just have to drop it down the
          hatch.

He passes her the canister. She holds it as
gingerly as a hot potato. Gives a nervous glance
at the hole in the wall.

                    HALDINE
          Pop it right in.

She pushes it through.

                    MARVELL
          And that's it?

                    HALDINE
          That's all you need to do.

A high pitched beeping sound emits from the
speaker. MARVELL jumps. The word BLOCKED flashes on
the screen.

                    HALDINE
          Oh, unless that happens.

                    CAIRNS
          That fucker's jamming all the time
          recently.

                    MARVELL
          I'm sorry.

                    HALDINE
          Don't worry, it's nothing you did. As
          far as I know. Press the eject button
          and start again.

She presses where he points, the canister emerges,
and HALDINE pushes it promptly back in again. The
word CLEARED flashes on screen.

MARVELL is amazed. She attempts to walk round

the machine, as though she's checking behind the magician's curtain.

HALDINE pulls her back.

> HALDINE
> Oh, health and safety. Better not do that in case a canister tears through you at the speed of light.

CAIRNS rolls her eyes.

> MARVELL
> Wow. That's so cool. I can't believe they just - go. Where's it gonna turn up?

> HALDINE
> The ones in this machine all go to the same spot, twenty miles from here. Just this morning a canister arrived that we sent twelve months ago. I'll take you over some time.

> MARVELL
> I'd like that.

> HALDINE
> It's an exciting time to start working here. We know we can send objects into the future, and it's getting further all the time.

> MARVELL
> So what do you do with the stuff that people send back?

> HALDINE
> Back from where?

> MARVELL
> The future.

HALDINE's eyes flicker towards CAIRNS. She keeps looking at the newspaper.

> HALDINE
> That never happens.

CAIRNS slaps her right arm onto the table.

It's a prosthetic.

HALDINE glances at CAIRNS again. But MARVELL continues; CAIRNS is not in her eyeline.

>   MARVELL
> Oh. Well that must be really
> disappointing.
>
>   HALDINE
> Disappointing? No, no, not at all.
>
>   MARVELL
> But if you were really making contact,
> wouldn't you have heard from someone in
> the future by now?

HALDINE looks relieved. There's a standard answer for this.

>   HALDINE
> That's a common misunderstanding. There's
> a thing called the Chronology Protection
> Conjecture. You can't travel backwards
> in time.
>
>   MARVELL
> Yeah, yeah I know about that.
>   (sing-song)
> "Nature always prevents time travel that
> will cause a paradox."
>   (normal)
> What about when there's no paradox?

CAIRNS laughs and stands up. From among the papers littering the table she takes a slim booklet with the company logo on the cover. Crosses the room. Stands between MARVELL and HALDINE.

>   CAIRNS
> Read that. No need for him to waste his
> breath on the company line.

MARVELL takes the booklet. CAIRNS reaches past her, to press the speaker button.

SPEAKER
Central headquarters.

CAIRNS
There's mice in this building. If you
don't want them to chew through the wires
of your forty-six million pound computer,
you need to start laying poison.

SPEAKER
Thank-you Cairns.

CAIRNS walks out.

HALDINE
I think I can leave you to this now.

INT. SECURITY ROOM. DAY

A wall of screens. A SECURITY GUARD sleeps in his
chair. CAIRNS is watching the flickering images.
One in particular. The courtyard. Except now it is
full of people: lab technicians. They congregate
as a canister materialises.

SECURITY GUARD
(His eyes are shut)
Still waiting for that arm to arrive?

CAIRNS lights a cigarette, and keeps watching.

INT. LAB/BASEMENT. DAY

MARVELL checks a sheaf of papers, and looks at the
clock.

Retrieves a canister from the drawer.

Date stamps it, posts it through the hole.

The screen flashes CLEARED.

MARVELL
All right.

She sits at the table, pleased with herself.

INT. SECURITY ROOM. DAY

The courtyard on the screen is empty now. CAIRNS looks away.

                    CAIRNS
          See you later Jeff.

The SECURITY GUARD waves, his eyes still shut, as she walks away.

INT. LAB/BASEMENT. DAY

MARVELL is startled again by the high pitched beep of the machine alarm.

The screen reads BLOCKED.

MARVELL looks confused. She pushes the eject button. The beeping continues.

INT. CORRIDOR. DAY

CAIRNS stops at a drinks machine. She removes a finger from her prosthetic and uses the spoke to jimmy the lock.

INT. LAB/BASEMENT. DAY

MARVELL squints at the hole. Her hand advances towards it.

CAIRNS taps her on the shoulder.

                    CAIRNS
          I wouldn't risk that if I were you.

She is holding a steaming paper cup, which she offers to MARVELL.

                    CAIRNS
          Thought you could do with a coffee by now.

                    MARVELL
          Thanks. I'm so glad you're back. I don't
          know what's the matter with this thing.

                    CAIRNS
          It blocks all the time.

                    MARVELL
          But there's no canister in there. The
          last one cleared twenty minutes ago.

                    CAIRNS
          Huh.

She reaches in with her prosthetic.

                    MARVELL
          Are those things expensive?

                    CAIRNS
          Yes.

Her arm is in up to the elbow. Face creased with concentration. Her eyes widen and she suddenly withdraws.

                    CAIRNS
          That's too soft for a canister. I can
          tell from the grip.

                    MARVELL
          I'll call Central HQ.

                    CAIRNS
                    (angered)
          No! Don't.

She immediately re-inserts her prosthetic. Takes a deep breath. Pulls as hard as she's able.

A baby, red and squalling, slithers from the machine.

MARVELL drops the cup of coffee and screams.

                    CAIRNS
                    (to the baby)
          It's OK. It's OK.

CAIRNS is breathing fast but otherwise calm. She carries the baby to the table and lies her flat.

                    CAIRNS
          Take your jumper off.

MARVELL removes her sweater with shaking hands.
She is close to tears.

> MARVELL
> Who puts a baby in a time machine?

CAIRNS takes the garment and wraps it round the
baby.

> CAIRNS
> Someone who's scared of the future.

> MARVELL
> It wasn't us who did this?

CAIRNS' expression is contemptuous. She shakes her
head.

> CAIRNS
> She look much like a tin can to you?

> MARVELL
> So who?

> CAIRNS
> It could be anyone in the next five
> hundred years. That's as far as we've
> opened the time streams.

> MARVELL
> Haldine said it wasn't possible to send
> things backwards.

> CAIRNS
> Haldine talks a lot of shit.

> MARVELL
> I'm calling Central HQ.

> CAIRNS
> No!

MARVELL has already pushed the button. CAIRNS
scoops the baby up and pushes in front: an attempt
at damage limitation.

> SPEAKER
> Central HQ.

> CAIRNS
> This is Cairns. We have a code 16.

> SPEAKER
> Specify the object.

> MARVELL
> A baby.

> SPEAKER
> I'm sorry, could you say that again?

> CAIRNS
> (sighs)
> A baby girl. She has no visible scars, and the bomb detector has not gone off. How should we proceed?

The baby cries while they wait for a response.

> SPEAKER
> Please follow the normal procedure.

> CAIRNS
> You can't be serious.

> SPEAKER
> Haldine is on his way to oversee her return.

> MARVELL
> See, they know where she's from.

CAIRNS looks at her in disbelief.

She strides with the baby towards the corridor.

INT. CORRIDOR DAY

CAIRNS makes it to the far end. HALDINE stands in the doorway.

> HALDINE
> I've brought security with me.

> CAIRNS
> You think I can't get past Jeff?

HALDINE steps forward. The guard behind him is a big guy, and armed. CAIRNS sags. The baby cries.

INT. LAB/BASEMENT. DAY

CAIRNS listens to the baby cry as everyone crowds round the machine. She keeps her back to them, unable to watch.

A translucent, protective shell now encases the baby. MARVELL raises her to the hole. HALDINE adjusts dials.

CAIRNS closes her eyes. The crying stops. There is silence.

> SPEAKER
> Could all three lab technicians please report to Webb's office.

HALDINE looks at MARVELL. She gives a small nod, but then glances warily at CAIRNS. They all wait for her acknowledgement.

> SPEAKER
> Hello? Cairns? Cairns? Cairns?

CAIRNS takes her time. MARVELL, HALDINE, JEFF, and the armed guard are frozen. She leans into the microphone.

> CAIRNS
> Go screw yourself.

INT. WAITING ROOM. DAY

HALDINE and MARVELL wait to be called into the boss's office like schoolchildren expecting punishment. Clutched in HALDINE's hand is a rumpled printout that he keeps trying to smooth.

> MARVELL
> How could you tell where the baby was from?

> HALDINE
> (uncomfortable)
> We never know where Code 16s are from.

> MARVELL
> So where did you dispatch her?

> HALDINE
> I followed procedure. All Code 16s are dispatched to the limit of the time stream.

> MARVELL
> Cairns said you wouldn't send her home... I just thought she was nuts.

She looks like she might be sick.

The boss's secretary approaches them with a smile. The post-mortem awaits.

INT. WEBB'S OFFICE. DAY

A sleek room in the sky. Clean lines. Chrome. Empty space.

By the window stands a suited man: WEBB. He is motionless, watchful and as cold as his surroundings.

This only heightens how drained and disheveled HALDINE and MARVELL look.

> HALDINE
> (coughing)
> The Code 16 was resolved. I dispatched the object to the year 2539. Cairns was, ah, customarily obstructive.

He rustles his sheaf of papers. MARVELL rubs her eyes.

WEBB observes people milling on the street far below. He smiles; honey tinged with sulphur.

> WEBB
> Fine. Go.

They make for the door.

WEBB turns and points at MARVELL.

                    WEBB
          Not you.

                    MARVELL
          I don't know anything. In fact - I'd
          really like to just go home now?

                    WEBB
                    (to HALDINE)
          On your way out, tell Carmela to bring
          refreshments.

HALDINE nods and exits. WEBB remains at the
window. He gestures to a chair which MARVELL -
hesitantly - takes. She avoids his gaze by looking
at his glass desk. No personal effects.

                    WEBB
          You've had an interesting first day.

                    MARVELL
          I've had an interesting last day. I feel
          like a...I feel like a criminal.

                    WEBB
          This wasn't a crime. My remit is to
          protect our country's security. When we
          operate time machines, we become border
          guards.

                    MARVELL
          How can a baby threaten security? You
          talk like she was some kind of bomb.

                    WEBB
          She may have been.

                    MARVELL
          I'm not cut out for this job.

                    WEBB
          Marvell. No one ever leaves here.

She takes a handkerchief from her pocket and
twists it between her fingers.

                    MARVELL
               What happened to Cairns' arm?

WEBB finally sits down.

                     WEBB
               I believe she sustained a war injury.

                    MARVELL
               Who paid for the prosthetic?

His secretary glides into the office, bearing a
tray which she places between them.

                     WEBB
               You'd need to ask Cairns. Tea?

                    MARVELL
               No, I -

She stops, and stares at the teapot CARMELA is
pouring. It is ceramic, curlicued and ruby-red.
Alarmingly red, in the iciness of WEBB's office.
Like a drop of blood in snow.

The tea cascades into a matching cup. CARMELA
places it before WEBB and retreats.

                    MARVELL
               This place is not what I expected.

                     WEBB
               You knew we employ people for life. Why
               did you apply here?

                    MARVELL
               Corny reasons. Naive. I thought I could
               do some good.

                     WEBB
               How?

                    MARVELL
               It doesn't matter now, because I'm
               leaving.

WEBB hasn't touched the tea.

MARVELL
That's a very unusual tea set.

WEBB
It's a family heirloom.

MARVELL
I have one exactly the same at home. I thought it was the only one.

WEBB smiles at her attempt to distract him. But it's a proper smile, a sunshine in April smile, that changes his whole appearance.

WEBB
Why did you want to work with us? I'd really like to know.

MARVELL
Well...

She sighs, and looks around her. There's a blue-and-grey Rothko. Empty glass vases, regimented, on a shelf.

Her eyes settle on the tea tray. A scarlet plate is adorned with petit fours.

She lines the cakes along the desk.

MARVELL
These are all the people in the world. All using oil. All competing for agricultural land. All rioting over food and having as many little cake babies as they can.

She splays her fingers flat on the glass. In one go, gently, she nudges every alternate cake an inch forward.

There are now two rows.

MARVELL
Lets say half of these people can skip
forward in time a year. And the day they
arrive, the other half leap forward in
time to the year after that.

WEBB
You immediately halve the number of
people using resources at any one point.

WEBB pushes the tea cup towards MARVELL. He takes
a petit four and balances it at the edge of the
saucer. This time she does not protest.

MARVELL
Somehow I doubt you're interested in
sustainability.

She bites the cake, almost absent-mindedly.

WEBB
I've looked into leapfrogging. But that
doesn't exclude other commercial and
military applications.

MARVELL
I don't want to help the military. I
don't want to send babies into the
unknown because you think they're a
terrorist threat.

WEBB
Wars have to be won.

MARVELL
We're not at war.

WEBB
We will always be at war now. A future
enemy can take aim down the time stream
whenever they like.

MARVELL
I'd rather take that risk than hurt
innocent children.

WEBB
You're right. You are naive.

MARVELL
I just don't believe you can achieve anything good by evil means.

WEBB
You're also not entirely honest.

MARVELL
Excuse me?

WEBB
About your motives.

MARVELL
I don't understand.

WEBB
Imagine someone you care about is ill. Maybe a genetic illness. Something progressive.

MARVELL
OK.

She fixates on the half-full tea cup in front of her.

WEBB
You don't have to imagine it, do you?

MARVELL
That isn't any of your business.

WEBB
So this illness. It strikes you when you're old enough to already have kids, and does it's worst before they've grown up.

MARVELL is growing agitated.

WEBB
Except... if you have a time machine... you can see them grow up...

                    MARVELL
          You've done a lot of research. Is it only
          my mother you've looked into? Perhaps
          you'd like to say something about my
          drunken father, too?

WEBB is inscrutable.

                    MARVELL
          Jesus.

She stands.

                    MARVELL
          You're disgusting.

She can't leave fast enough.

                    WEBB
          Carmela will box the cakes.

                    MARVELL
          I don't like them. I hate them, actually.

                    WEBB
          That isn't true.

She ignores him.

                    WEBB
          I understand, Marvell. My wife is sick.

A waver. She pauses half way out the door.

                    MARVELL
          Then I feel sorry for you. I still don't
          want this job.

                    WEBB
          Wanting is neither here nor there. No
          one ever leaves.

They stare at each other.

But she breaks away first.

She's gone; the door closes.

WEBB presses an intercom button on his desk.

                    WEBB
            No further calls today.

                  INTERCOM
    Noted.

He stands up. Still. Stares at the Rothko.

Reverently, he draws nearer and nearer. He lifts away the canvas.

Underneath is another time machine. Another incandescent, shining halo.

But a grown man could escape through this one.

                    WEBB
            Oh, I could look into you for hours.

The machine purrs.

WEBB turns one hundred and eighty degrees.

He falls backwards.

Into the depths.

                                        FADE OUT:

GEOFF MILLS woke up from a troubled dream one morning to find himself transformed in his bed into a terrible cliché.

"A writer? In a garret? In London? With not a penny to my name? How about if I sleep a bit longer and forget all this nonsense," he thought.

And so he did.

A Rat's Tale
by Geoff Mills

Allow me to introduce myself. My name is Doctor Dominic du Mortier and I am a hundred and sixty one years old. No, no, stay where you are please. It's not that I'm unwilling to shake your hand, please don't think that. It's really more a case of my being unable. Permit me to explain.

I am beyond reach. And behind glass. And a rodent. Nothing special you understand – just a *Rattus norvegicus*, or a common brown rat to you.

Oh yes, and dead. Did I mention that? Well then. There you have it.

Too much to take in? Hard to swallow? Well naturally it is! How do you think *I* felt? I've had almost two centuries to get used to the idea. And I haven't. I wasn't always what I am now, you understand? A sentient streak of fur. I was like you, once. I walked I whistled, I danced I dreamed, I feared I fucked. I had a wife, a boy, a house in Hampstead. Life was fine. Health wise I was getting along OK, no complaints there. I was perhaps a little on the portly side, but nothing a few months jogging wouldn't sort out. And there were the arthropods, of course, my professional if peculiar *raison d'etre*.

Perhaps you've perused the section I used to preside over at the museum? Many people do, while they sojourn in London. If you haven't already I would recommend you drop in on my friends, the Creepy Crawlies, on the ground floor. You can't miss them: Dippy the Diplodocus was always kind enough to point them out with his double beamed, double-decker length tale. That is, if he's standing in the same place. I sometimes forget how long it's been. Time flies, you see, when you're stiff with boredom. Or bored with stiffness.

What happened? Well I became the cliché. I became *that man*. I was walking to work one fine day (yes, I *was* whistling now you ask), just about the time our great city was gearing up for the arrival of the Olympics, and I found myself being charged down by some foreign fool on a Boris bike. I stepped aside nimbly enough, only to be hit squarely in the back by a Boris *bus*. Whack, crack, splat. Well, it did for me you see. Not straight away, but eventually. Fractures and ruptures all over the body shop. I mean Boris was a splendid sort of chap, with some decent enough ideas on transport, but if I'd have known *that* was going to happen, I would never have squandered my vote on him.

While Boris was enjoying his second term in office, buzzing around in his barmy busy bee way, I was rotting vegetatively in bed while staring at the one thing that sat in my eye line. Me. Or at least, what I am now. God knows why they had it in a hospital – even if it was private. It must surely have breached some code of hygiene if not of taste. But there I was, in my little glass tomb, staring back at myself, so that I became him as much as I was I, and he me as much as he was he. How could I not? How could *he* not? We spent three years staring into each other's eyes, for god's sake! Child of the Enlightenment that I was I just couldn't resist this compelling metaphysical leap.

Don't look at me like that! You think I'm mad, don't you? Well of course I am. My head was hit by ten tons of bus! I was incarcerated within my own body for thirty-seven months, and now I've been trapped inside a rat's body for a hundred and sixty one years! You want to try being where I am *now*.

Well anyway, I passed on. My wife pulled the plug, in a kind way. She murdered me tenderly. My son was sat on the bed; playing with the stuffed souvenir Dippy I had given him on his fourth birthday. The last thing I saw, in my earthly guise at least, was the top of that poor boy's head and those rat's eyes boring their way into my brain, my soul. And the last thing I heard was the flat lining of the ECG around which Emily's sobs wove a quavering tune, and Thomas whispering calmly into Dippy's ear. "Daddy's going to heaven now. Daddy's going to heaven."

* * *

What do I remember of my second life? I recall a diminishing darkness, a dispersing fog, and a slowly resolving vision of the bed from which I had risen. That some time had passed since my passing I could sense, but would have surmised in any case for now the room lay in a state of crude dismantlement. The fittings had been ripped away, the flooring torn up, the furniture removed and a jagged doorway torn through into a neighbouring bathroom. My bed, shorn of its mattress and rudely disrobed, stood four legged, naked and squat on the stripped floor. On its steel back had been dumped a box of tools, several rolls of wallpaper, some crushed drinks cans and a tinny little radio that seemed to be screeching out with interminable pain.

So enthralled, so transfixed, so mesmerised was I by the brutal disintegration, the gradual reconstruction of my visual universe that it little occurred to me to question the actuality of my actualness, the indubitable undeadness of my dead state. Astonishingly, in those early years, I accepted without demur the fact that my consciousness had inhabited the body of the glaring rat, seemed to take for granted that somehow, in a way that was beyond my paltry understanding, the laws of cause and effect had taken their natural course. With a wonder verging on the infantile I gaped unblinkingly on as men laboured, suits inspected, maids in monochrome flurried and fussed, and the room was made fabulous with fabrics then soft and spruce with cushions in pastel. But the crowning touch was *this*, delivered in sections and then built, over a day, into an emperor sized, faux-Tudor, four-poster canopied bed.

Well, imagine my position. No, I mean my actual physical location. For it is this, you understand, which locks down my line of sight and so defines the physical boundaries of my universe.

For some reason, after a vigorous polishing of the glass that enclosed me, and a lower refitting of the shelf upon which my glass home rested, it was decided that I was an acceptable part of the *mise en scène* - that I was to be saved the indignities of deposal, disposal or destruction. So now, I repeat: imagine my position. Place yourself in my pelt. Where am I? What do I see?

Exactly! I had been given a front row seat at the theatre of debauch. I had been dropped into the stalls, had no choice but to play witness to the night action of the stage. It had even been framed by a proscenium arch then salaciously draped with curtains of crimson. Oh how I laughed! What odd purgatory was this? What peculiar hinterland had I been cast into?

Where do I begin? Do I begin at all? Who else but a cursèd few have witnessed two centuries worth of couplings and copulations, carnality and coitus? I have seen tender, milk skinned virgins deflowered by fumbling youths and slavering predators. I have seen wedding nights bungled by clueless Christians and the comically mismatched. I have seen marriages broken the night they were made; marriage proposals made and unmade; marriage vows shattered - casually, callously, casuistically. I have seen wholesome threesomes, and fulsome foursomes; in all configurations. I have seen queer quintets, tantric contortionists and pensioners at play. I have seen muscle men mastered by diminutive maids, and fragile frames mounted by monsters.

I have heard whimpers and simpers, screams, screeches and squawks. I have seen flops, failures and fatal faux pas. I have seen Greek love, Sapphic love; self, selfless and selfish love. I have heard the post-coital sighs of the oppressed, the depressed and the impressed. I have seen them in action fully dressed, half dressed, cross dressed, dressed up or conventionally undressed; stood up, stretched out or suspended from the chandelier. In natural light, candle light, with the houselights glaring and the houselights snuffed. You would be surprised how much goes on in total darkness: Braille lust? Though my perceptions are human, I have inherited the nocturnal habits as well as the night vision of the rat.

You assume, don't you, that I'm alone in all this? That I'm a solo spectator, a solitary voyeur? Of course you do, why would you think otherwise? For the first seventy-eight years I was of the same opinion. But this twisted plot performed yet another twiddle. I started to hear supernumerary voices: outbursts of surprise or satisfaction, revulsion or indifference. These so often concurred with my own turn of mind that I supposed them aural manifestations of my own damaged consciousness. But then these sounds, all with distinct tones and emerging from seemingly unique personalities, began to evolve into verbalizations. These, I was intrigued and even delighted to discover, were often at variance with my own, and even more so with each other. For a few days I listened to the feuding, glad of the diversion; but one evening, before I was even aware, I found myself drawn into debate with them.

The exchange concerned the sexual proclivities of a young Polish lady, who insisted on being struck hard in the body and face as a kind of *appetiser* to the main course, which given the girth of her bedfellow would have been a meaty dish indeed. Now this brutish-looking fellow found himself discomfited by her increasingly shrill commands and, though he obliged to a degree, found he couldn't quite bring himself to hit her as hard as his strength would allow. He had dealt controlled slaps to the face, and rather half hearted blows to the stomach, but she was growing manic and blotchy in her calls for an escalated violence. Perhaps to provoke him into action she curled up her dainty fists and swung them roundly into the large man's face, again and again and again. Had he reciprocated she would surely have crumbled, instead of which he caught her flailing wrists in his paws, grumbled some words of regret, gathered up his things and left.

Our debate was hindered somewhat by the concatenation of

high-pitched obscenities the little Angelika was flinging down the corridor, but concerned the ethical issues raised by the event and conjecture as to whether we ourselves could have acquiesced to her deviant injunction. Only when the heat had evaporated from our exchange did I care to enquire who the hell I was talking to.

Well, what can I say? I was as surprised as anyone! They had always been there, you understand; we had just never spoken. I didn't know we *could*. I had assumed their sullen silence was a matter of simple physics: they were stuffed animals for heaven's sake! Yes I know, what hypocrisy! Why would I be the *one* exception to the rule? But I had been among my own all that time.

Allow me to introduce. Here is Sam Thomson, formerly an airline pilot but currently, as you can see, appearing in the rather splendid form of the *Sciurus Vulgaris*, or red squirrel to the layman. Heart attack midair at forty-five. Then there's Dora Ravensdale, a splendid example of a *Muscardinidae*, or dormouse, heretofore a primary school teacher in Slough. Don't concern yourself too much with her – she's napping, as she so often does. Natural causes, before you ask. Her girlfriend nudged her off the top floor of an NCP, so naturally she died. Directly behind her – can you see ok? - is Brian Perdue, killed in action whilst on a tour of duty in Northern Ireland. He appears - despite his conspicuous lack of sagacity, forgive me Brian! - in the form of a *Tyto alba*, or common barn owl. And of course who could forget dear old Harriet Howsham, who was a grandmother to eight and baker of cakes *par excellence* when she passed through into her present incarnation. If you note her grey-brown hair and the distinct absence of a cute little cotton tail you will of course conclude that she is an *Oryctolagus cuniculus,* or European Rabbit. She nodded off in front the television one evening and never woke up. Prime time TV could do that to you, in those days.

Our existence is largely anodyne, wouldn't you know? Not for us the pain of mere existence, or overmuch contemplation of our strange hinterland continuation. We nap, we chatter; we doze we natter. Dislocated from physical or spiritual want, we repose comfortably in a state of trivial contentment. We are brains in a jar, our formaldehyde spiked with Soma or some such, our eyes attached to stalks and suckered to the outside. Certainly we dream, mostly of our past and sometimes of our future lives. And we have the comings and goings of these silly sex-crazed ninnies to keep us vaguely amused. There is nothing sexual in it for *us*, you realize, not even of a vicarious kind. Scopophiliacs we are not: the sensual urgings expired with our flesh. For us these night time activities have become a kind of unavoidable spectator sport: a matter for dispassionate notice, cynical censure, ironic comment. And though it may seem from my narrative that this coterie has done nothing but feast on fornication, you must acknowledge that ninety eight percent of bed action is dull *in*action: spooning, squabbling, snoozing, snoring.

From our viewing angle the configuration of the room has remained essentially the same, although over the years we have been presented with a kaleidoscopic array of designs. In its latest manifestation the space has been upgraded into something of a ritzy presidential suite. Now this was a real *coup* and transformed overnight the quality of our actors entirely. Oh believe me when I say that we have seen the honey trappings of power, the intimate organs of church and state, the infamies and misfortunes of fame and fortune. The most important person this room has hosted, you ask? Well now, thank you for asking! And so fortuitously too, for I was about to embark on a tale of a most powerful gentleman.

The greater the man the greater the hullaballoo preceding his arrival. On this occasion more security sweeps have been conducted on the room than I care to throw a cliché at. The US Secretary for State arrives late one evening on a gust of self importance, amid a cloud of his own flatulence, half cut and with a family sized bucket of sweat dribbling down his fat senatorial face. He has a garishly trussed up, six foot odd, ebony skinned prostitute in tow, whom he leads to the bed and sacrifices gruntingly to Aergia, the goddess of sloth. The next day he schleps his corpulent form out of bed, washes two fried breakfasts down with a litre of bourbon and belches his way out of the room. He returns later that evening with a pretty girl on his arm. She looks around eighteen; perhaps younger, perhaps older. He is drunk, she is drunker. She is shrilly giggling, careening about the place, her blonde locks falling about her unblemished, creamy white face. He is ordering wine from the downstairs bar with a liquid drawl half Texan, half pissed, dimming the lights, selecting music for the moment, unsheathing her slowly with his porcine eyes.

Later, he opens the bathroom door to find her dancing, eyes closed, jauntily, arhythmically - perhaps to a beat of her own imagining. A silver tray lies by the bed – on it sits an empty bottle of Griotte-Chambertin, a gleaming corkscrew and two empty glasses rubescently stained.

He takes off his jacket, his tie and approaches the girl, his right arm stretching out to touch her curls, his toxic breath melting over her face. Her eyes pop open, and she gasps and jerks backwards but he is on her, all over her, his seventeen stone pinning her against the bed and his right hand pulling at his trousers, her skirt and his left hand pressing down across her mouth and his acid tongue lapping at her face and she hears the wheezy roaring of his minotaur breath and her legs are jerking and twitching and her left arm is pushing against the crushing mass and her right arm is groping blindly towards the bottle, the glasses anything she can grasp and she feels a scalding numbness between her thighs and her fingers are closing round the cold steel and now she can see it quivering above her before she brings the sharp point down into the back of his neck and SCHLAM he is roaring and screaming and arching up and clutching his neck and she is swinging the wet point of the corkscrew towards his face and

BANG drives it right through the side of his cheek so that for a second he can taste the edge of the screw on his tongue and she drags it back out and in and BANG right through the side of his eyeball so that he is screaming and sliding off the bed and on his back and blinded by the blood and she is above him and can feel this rage this rage this screaming rage and she drops to her knees and grasps the corkscrew in both hands and drives it down through his other eye then leans in so hard she can feel it pushing down through the resistant cheese of his brain.

Oh dear, I haven't made you queasy have I? It's not a pleasant story - that I will admit. You will have heard some of the details on the news I imagine, but not these. No, not these details. Imagine how it was for us, crying out clamorous yet unheard. Well the girl scarpered, made a run for it, as you would. If you could hear a single word of this I'd ask if you knew what came of her. You should have seen the scrum that followed. For the week or so this room was the centre of the world.

I've no idea what's going to happen now. To the room, that is, and consequently us. It's been locked up and out of use for a year or so. Maybe *you* would know? Who *are* you anyway? What are you *doing* here? Y'know, now I look at you more closely you remind me very much of someone I know. Yes, someone I know very well, I just can't put my claw on it. It'll come to me I'm sure. After I've slept perhaps. It must be the exhaustion, this exhaustion. Funny, I've never felt this tired before. You won't object if I sleep now, would you? You appear to be sleeping yourself in any case.

Yes, sleep. Oh Sleep. Tired nature's sweet restorer, restore me too.

* * *

And what I saw, as they turned that infernal machine off, was the top of my poor boy's head and those rat's eyes urging me, compelling me into life. And what I heard was the flat lining of the ECG around which Emily's sobs wove a quavering tune, and Thomas whispering calmly into Dippy's ear, "Daddy's going to heaven now. Daddy's going to heaven." And what I thought was "What's *this* nonsense?" and with a sheer effort of will I rose Lazarus-like from the bed, plucked the electrodes from my greying skin and pulled my loved ones close against me. And I smelt the hair of my beautiful boy, and I kissed the neck of my beautiful wife, and their warm life flowed into me and made me mortal again.

SHERYL PRIOR has recently completed a BA in English and Creative Writing at Birmingham City University, and will be progressing to a Masters in Writing in the autumn. This is her first published story.

A Fairy Tale
by Sheryl Prior

1.

There are crows on the roof. You can hear them clawing: scratch-tap, scratch-tap. They wake you up sometimes. Your mother says they're dancing, and you think of them in their glossy shoes. Once when your father took her over to the phone box, he tried to turn your back but you heard them first. Their cries were like sawing wood, stealing the flesh from the dead thing. Each beak, a tiny witch's hat, was spilling mauve strings, bloody knots. You pulled away easily from his hand. He said it was a baby, like you in your soft bootees. Its eyes were black and you saw something move inside.

Your sister is crying this morning. She has cut her thumb on a rusty nail outside. She sucks the bad blood out but doesn't stop. Too hungry: her thumb is turning blue so you must hold it from her. She clacks and snaps like Punch. Your sister is nearly a woman but your mother says she is a baby inside too. She laughs like a baby; that wet sickly hole opens like a flower.

And now she has left her stones and clots in your bed and they will stroke you sore tonight.

Pricking her finger with each stroke, your mother is sewing something lumpy and grey. She never wears a thimble and she can't hear the kettle sing, because it is screaming. When you look, there is no water in the kettle. Who turned on the gas?

It's so close outside. That's what they say, very close. It's closer inside, there's nothing but walls. All of them brown like dirt. There are only insects to play with.

Later, in the dark, you wait. Your mother washes herself in the only sink - the taps clunk. The water puts sand in the linen.

When she is done, you hear through the famished wall the creak of the bed that your mother shares with her eldest child. Now sleeping, your sister's jaws pump like a guppy's.

Your dirty feet stand straight at the foot of the bed like beaten standing-stones. The moon dangles shadows of crone's noses and twisted lips to share the walls with leafy boughs. And then *he* comes again. You can smell him first. That smell: like bare earth after the rain, and wood-smoke. There's meat there too: bare flesh, sweat and wounds.

And you hear the bells on him as he dances; the few bells that haven't dropped from the rotten strings.

You pull the cover up close. Breath sighs through the tears in it. You anticipate him with your drum-rolling heart.

He stops for a moment at the foot of the stairs and then climbs, relishing every step. For a moment he stops outside your door, but this time it's the other one he opens, to where your mother and sister lie. Their bed groans again to take him.

Your hands cradle your head but the pulse in your ears races and roars. You can hear his laughter, like water in your ears. Like the thump of birds on the soft grass. Like the screech owl. You are lying in marshland and it is forever before you hear him go.

In the morning you are the first to rise. Water hangs expectantly in the air outside. Wet leaves are like sleeping molluscs.

Sour milk pools in the gutters of saucepans left out. A spider cautiously tests a ledge of crusted remains. Under a towel, you find it. You put the knife in your bag, bread crumbs hide in its cruel grooves.

He sleeps all day and dances all night. He has haunted your dreams since before you saw your father on the barbed wire, and your mother said he'd slipped on the ice. There were no birds in the sky and your sister's mouth creaked on its hinge for days.

2.

Outside you stop on that patch of earth, the flat strip before the curling path that goes down, and down. Down into the wet, past the window with the teddy bears. You found a dead mouse on that path once. You held its corpse; bones swam underneath the silk. Its eyes had been taken, a shame your doll's were too big to fit.

The communal toilet block is black all over. The notice-board says the bus will come twice a week. The wall says Tracy gives good head. You can hear them inside: the other children laugh like they don't know about *him*.

Inside are the three boys and the girl with the hair like autumn. They lift her skirt like they might peel the shell from an egg. They don't want to look when you walk in the wet grass. When you breathe in, all the mucus lining the road to your brain splutters and pops.

You say tell me more. You need to know why you can't sleep. The tallest boy with the mismatched eyes has a mouth like a sickle. They are laughing, all of them. Circling like hyenas. The tall boy says *he* has the head of a sheep where the flesh has fallen from the bone, with mad eyes that look everyway at once. Dead flies dance on the air that defies the window frame. Glass the colour of set honey.

The next boy has dead arms that hang heavy. He tells you *he* has the body of a bear, with shit and fern in its matted hair - its human hair. He has the claws of a bear on its feet but the hands of a man, says the boy with the oversized tongue. Like a pillow, he can't keep it inside his cleft lip. And the girl, she laughs like the crows laughed. She knows he comes to you in the night when you're tucked up in bed and his hair scratches and his breath is like dead things and he kisses you again and again.

"It's gonna get you." They mean, it got your mother and that's why that sister of yours dribbles down herself when she sees a puppy dog.

How did something like that get born?

It was made by human hand. Sewn. Thrown together like a casserole. It's like a doll that comes to life: somebody loves it.

How do you kill something that is already dead?

I don't know.

How do you kill something that never lived?

You cut its legs off so that it can't walk. You cut its arms off so that it can't drag itself. You bury it in the peat swamp so that it can't fly and she won't find it.

The witch in the corner with the allotment, the one with breasts the size of the gourds outside number twenty-seven, that sit on her stomach like a pair of eyes roving over a nose. You know she is watching when you can smell what's between her legs. She takes him dead badgers when there are no human babies.

They say she can make anything. She used to make dresses for real ladies, before she lost her mind. Before that she made paper doilies with a pair of scissors. All she makes now is a lot of silence: silence that can pound your bones.

She'll tell you where he is. The mother knows the son. She knows him every night.

3.

So you go there.

When you get to the place the curtains are drawn in the front. A thick snail clings to the only leaf in the allotment. A thousand more cling to every stone and clot.

A voice like sandpaper on rust; she asks who is there but she knows. She saw you once in the toilet when they dared you to do it standing up, but they ran away. Her voice is dry but her mouth is wet.

She wears a man's t-shirt that once was white. There are tears around the neck and a stain like a teaspoon. Her arms at once bulge and sag like deflated balloons, browning like soft fruit. The hem of her pleated skirt curves like an eyelid; her knees smile underneath. She holds a wooden spoon like a sword and the furrows in her gut pulse open and shut contentedly with each rasping breath. She is asking about food, she has rusks for the baby, or porridge. She has jam but no bread.

You say yes, you are hungry. Your mother never told you not to talk to strangers.

The room smells of dead fish and machine oil. The tap drips. The old hag stands over a cot and sings. She sings something like Rock-A-Bye Baby but the words are wrong. She strains her lips to keep the sparse chips of tooth from slipping from her rotten gums. The hag tells you to help yourself to the food in the cupboards but she doesn't turn from the cot. When you stand up, the chair holds your shape. When you hold the arm to push from, there is a sticky brown stain on your palm and fingers.

The cupboards are mostly empty but for the clutter of spiders and cockroaches. You find biscuits that stick to your throat like sawdust and taste like the mouths of old men. The hag calls you back. She tries to sing it but the note she strikes is like a hammer on wood. The dozen dead pigeons in the flue make it hard to breathe right and she puts a fresh log in the fire at every twenty past the hour. There's a brocade codpiece hanging from a lampshade, and on the door a pile of coats deeper than wide. There is no door-handle.

The hag says "See this doll here? I made it for baby from every doll that she broke. See its hair? I want you to brush it through."

She gives it to you and a comb with one tooth.

The doll has one leg of six inches and one of twenty. Its face is like a hedgehog's she says, shitting glass you think. The hair is full of spit and cereals, hard in the shape of a love-heart.

You brush it.

Then the hag says "See this dress here? It was baby's christening gown but it got holes in it." The dress is made of lace. "Sew it up for baby."

She gives you the thread but she has lost the needle. It is in the carpet somewhere with the others.

You sew it.

Where is baby? That thing out of the cot, in the blue terry-towel romper, with a ferret for a bonnet. That thing, suckling the hag's mouldy tit. But then you see a cardboard box move.

You haven't asked her yet. That thing you see every night in your dreams. That gave your sister her rheumy eyes. The thing that wears bells on the edge of its cloak and bobs when it walks like it's wearing one high-heel. The thing that hasn't found you yet. Where is it?

Should she tell you? One more job. "Clean this rusty pot silver" - with a nail brush and stagnant toilet water.

No.

"What did you say?"

It can't be done. Water won't remove rust.

"What do you know? When I was your age I'd had ten babies. When I was your age I'd baked one blackbird into sixteen pies and it was still alive when my husband bit into it. The gravy could have done with more salt."

Fuck you.

"You'll have to pay. I charge 50p for the full works."

Where is he?

"Who?"

You know who.

"I don't know him. I can't remember his name but I saw him messing about with a plastic bow and arrow at that place where the brook takes a fork. Do you want tea?"

You say yes but your mouth is already wet with excitement. She gives you hot water with dirt in it but it's sweeter than candied peel.

How will the smoke get out? The smell of burnt hair will just cling to those coats like nobody's business when you throw her baby onto the fire. It's over there in that cardboard box by the tortoise with half a shell. Its body is like a kidney bean, body and head like a red blood cell from the side. It has arms in its clothes but where have its legs gone? And is there skin under that hair? You're not sure whether that thing is really a mouth, or a gash where it got caught in the door once. You think about her giving birth to it, pulling it out by the fur with her maggot fingers - glistening, slick.

The first time you throw it, it ricochets off the hood and into the downy teats of the sleeping Irish wolfhound. It doesn't wake up though, so it must be dead or comatose. You try again and this time it goes in. The hag has been waiting but her cry is still like a thousand elastic bands snapping at once, and a bit like pennies being dropped onto marble.

You run for the door but you forget there is no door handle. The hag isn't watching. She keeps putting her fingertips into the fire and pulling them out again when the blisters bubble high. The baby's hair goes up like a field mouse hibernating in a bonfire.

In the end you throw a fire extinguisher through the kitchen window and drop-roll onto the slabs.

You don't hear her say it was *his* baby.

It takes a while to climb up the embankment and into the woods. You're not sure if this is the way. Your knapsack has gone, and the bread-knife inside it, so you find a dead branch for a staff and wrap it in the barbed-wire that's lying about the forest floor. Yvonne was a lady who used to leave you lollies in the bucket by the front door. You call the stick Yvonne so that it won't scare you.

At the fork is a den. It's made out of white veneered chipboard and an old washing-machine but you look inside and there's no one there so you sit and wait. The sky is bleeding ink.

Is he coming? A baby deer stops in the clearing and looks at you. Its eyes are like chocolate buttons. It relieves itself and runs away. Far to your left you can see into the kitchen of the man with the dirty foam neck-brace that he's worn since before you were conceived. He told his wife that he was doing the washing up but you can see he's just dunking the mugs. In the distance you hear a cat being repeatedly kicked.

Then you hear the happy jangle, like a mobile toyshop. And a face like milk in the trees: the landlord's son in his plaid jacket and jeans and the cracked leather work-boots with the apple-red laces. He wears a look that tells you he's got no one to play with. Will you play with him? Will you swap your toy for his mouldy hobby-horse?

Tell him to go home. This isn't the time or place.

So he shakes his rotten toy and tries to hit you with his smelly hand with the over-long nails, with the dirt and maggot heads behind them. But you dodge his hand and hold your weapon between his eyes. Tell him you're not afraid to hurt him. He reminds you of your sister, the way he lashes out. Maybe *his* mother also knew the dead thing.

So he says ok. He's sorry and he'll be nice now and you believe him.

But you shouldn't.

He pushes you down and you lose. The man with the neck brace is watching over the sink as the landlord's son straddles your back. You can smell his awful hands. Your face is in the leaves and the dirt. Worms slide under your eyes like fleshy streamers and a train of woodlice burrow up into your brain. His sharp arse chisels away at the small of your back. His hands are pushing your palms into the peat. You are just below now, like a raisin at the surface of a fruit-cake.

He says you are bad. His baby is cold without its hair, and something moves in the darkness, smelling of burn. He pulls out your hand and plunges it into a warm and moist scabby lump that makes a sound like a cannon ball skimming water, and pulls away from you. You wriggle like a grub, but his sinews are iron ropes.

You hear a falcon swoop and then his grip is slack and your neck is wet, and hot. It drips from your hair. His blood showers from the sky and your sister, so tall in shoes with hard soles, swings your father's axe down like a baby-doll. You didn't lock the door when you left this morning.

You take the axe from her hand easily but you have to hold her back when you throw it into the trees. Your sister is stronger so you slap her face and launch the flesh like a pendulum. The axe falls on a roof somewhere, screaming.

The landlord's son lies in the mulch like he's sleeping there.

Your sister's skirt is pulled so high you can almost see her underwear. When you try to pull it down something lands on the soft earth like a butterfly. You see it first and try to reach it but your sister screams and spits like a cat. With the note, you push her face away and she snarls. You open the paper: it is torn writing paper smeared with earth. Faint, a drawing- a shape. A long head, gaping nostrils and sooty eyes; great spikes shoot upwards. Its bleached claws, inverted tree roots, clutch at nothing.

You, you say. You made this.

Your sister is silent: she is pretending to be dead. She is not dead - her pulse rocks you sitting on her back like a ragdoll on a bull. You hold it up to the last light of the sun and you see him there exactly as you've seen him a hundred times before, or more. You cannot count that high. His bone-lips sneer.

It is dusk. Shadows stain your pale face and your sister tries to lick them away until you shout. You hold the drawing over firm leaves and rip it again and again in the air till dandruff falls from your hands. Your sister pretends not to watch through glossy lashes. She called him on this way: but it was the landlord's son who answered. Now, he's lying down there like a leaky water bed. Your cheeks are hot and you want to leave her here, to tell your mother she must be lost. You pull her from the earth and let her feet drag until she stops. She won't walk any more. She wants you to carry her but she's too big and her belly is swollen like a peach. Why has she arched her back? Her wild eyes buck and you follow them to the trees but see nothing. When you look back she has gone with the swaying grass.

You move your feet again and you hear it. Wind through branches. Roaches in the dead trees. *Dancing bells.*

After recently completing an MA in Writing, RHODA THOMPSON is now writing a full-length collection of short and very short stories *Behind the Flowered Curtain* – one of which has achieved second place in the international flash fiction writing competition Flash500. She is also working on a creative non-fiction project *Dogs in the Family*.

Dance the Ghost with Me
by Rhoda Thompson

My reflection. Halloween party perfect: black hat topping scrags of witchety hair - with matching dress and floaty poncho cape. A face chock full of crooked teeth, grinning with a grimace instead a cackle.

The food waiting in the kitchen for all of them to mount: mini sandwich platters, chicken drumsticks and a large chocolate trifle - jammed together lumps of sweaty cheese. Requisite cans of beer and cider, as well as wine in trinity, that will go down easily and wash it all away.

Touching up ill-worn make-up while the radio bleats: muffles, waffles. It segues seamlessly into our song.

Eyes squinting out of the darkness, my head tilts in a sway. He comes up behind me then, but doesn't cause a start. Black-tie perfect. Dressed for a dinner party. Dressed to impress.

Gently, he removes the witch's hat and rests his scratchety beard there, his close-cut moustache bristling with something new. Placing sturdy arms over my tiny ones, he softly rocks with me while the song's beauty hangs about the room. We sit, together, joined in reflection.

I turn away from the mirror, and into eyes that are all his own. They are blue and brave, and braced for tears to match those falling from me.

"I miss him you know, you're so like him," a strange old lady speaks.

"I miss him too Nan but we've got to get a move on. The funeral cars are downstairs; waiting to take us to the church."

DAVID WAKE is an award-winning writer and director for the stage, and has trod the boards as Hamlet, Richard III, various policemen and the TV drama innovator, Rod Serling. As a stage manager, he's toured, gone to the Edinburgh fringe, been frozen in a fridge and lit Hollywood stars.

He's the New Writing Co-ordinator at the Blue Orange Theatre, Birmingham, where he runs the script development group.

See www.davidwake.com for more information about this and about his novella, *The Other Christmas Carol*, which is available on Amazon - it's never too early to buy a Christmas present.

Hang up
by David Wake

There were two of them: it was like they were breeding, and there was nothing wrong with his old mobile.

His apartment even had a landline, a neat reproduction of a Bakelite classic with a built-in answering machine and its buttons arranged like an antiquated dial. It sat on the Davenport, a little table designed for the purpose, in the hall with enough space for a fancy desk light with a green glass surround, a letter rack for the morning's mail and a bowl to take his keys and loose change. That's what he liked: a place for everything and everything in its place.

The red 'message received' light blinked for attention.

Conversation, for example, should be assigned a proper time and place without some chirping killjoy announcing yet another interruption. Romantic restaurants and bed were where you whispered sweet nothings to your girlfriend, Christmas and birthdays were when you talked to family, and Friday evenings down the pub were for friendly banter with your mates. Calls and texts at all hours were just demonstrations of insecurity: I need to be loved, I need to be loved, I need to be loved...

There was a time and a place.

And now everything had been shoved to one side to make room for two boxes, each proclaiming indispensible features. This chrome one, for example, had more megapixels than the digital camera that he'd been given two birthdays ago; whereas the black model had more megapixels than the digital SLR he'd had to buy because his mother had misunderstood his hints about cameras in the first place.

He pressed the 'play' button: "You have two new messages," said the cheerful automaton.

So, he never rang because his old phone couldn't take any more numbers, he'd said, and, ah, er... it was a work phone. But, contested his mother, when you were seven years old, your Father and I taught you to recite your home phone number in case anything happened to you. Yes, he admitted, but there were all the extra codes to add now. Occasionally, out of love and exasperation, she rang him. It was too rude to hang up, so he'd developed the knack of opening beer bottles and killing zombies with the Playstation on mute, while all the time listening to whatever it was that Mrs. Wotnot at Number 17 did... and had he heard about Mr. Thing... and there was So-and-So, you'd never guess...

He'd nodded and mumbled, and said "oh yes" once too often and she'd delivered the coup de grace: should she buy him a new phone, one that would store a million numbers, so he could program her into his favourites *and* set a reminder for every Sunday – but not during Gardeners' Question Time: do consider others, Keith, honestly!

"Message one."

"Keith, dear, did you get your new phone? Was it delivered? You can test it by calling me-"

"Oh for f-"

"Message deleted."

The other present was because he'd waited at the 'wrong' Japanese restaurant for an hour. As he'd stood there in the cold, a text had hung in the ether waiting for his phone to pick it up. If it had arrived, it would have explained to 'K' that he should be '@rd drgn gr8 place CU' and there he would find his girlfriend, 'Sxxx'. At the same time, Shirley had been called by an oh-so-understanding friend and so they'd met for cocktails. Men! Honestly! They were such bastards, as her friend had delighted in reminding Shirley in between gossip and sloe-comfortable-screws-against-the-wall in fancy glasses with umbrellas. The fact that he'd been at the correct restaurant did not excuse his thoughtlessness, particularly when he'd proved this by showing her the text she'd sent him. How dare he forgive her for the error - what was she, she demanded, some ditz who couldn't navigate?

Logically, she should have bought herself a SatNav, but oh no, the solution was a new phone for him: black, shiny, expensive and packed in a box far larger than the simple lozenge of technology needed. Now, she said, he could keep in touch; after all, he didn't want to make the same mistake again, did he? Well, no, he didn't, but he also didn't want to be on the end of a dangling string that stretched across base stations and therefore constantly at her beck and call. Your old phone doesn't work, she'd said, and it is the twenty first century, you know – duuur!

"Message two."

"Keith, what do you think of your new phone... I'm calling him... I'm calling him now... Shhhh, Tanya! I'm on the phone!"

He started ripping the cellophane off, tugged at the cardboard and... stupid things.

Hang on, his 'old' mobile was a twenty first century model.

He left the half-opened boxes on the Davenport and wandered about the flat. Out of the triple-gazed window of his city apartment, the twenty first century hurtled past below him lit in a vivid neon. It was all there: the solitary figures hunched over their phones as they texted similar monastic souls, the screeching hen-parties all dressed in the same outrageous individuality as they hectored absent friends on their phones and the mad blokes talking to themselves as they swaggered around complete with ear piece and microphone like spies on a secret mission. People who talked to themselves in the street used to be locked up.

He just wanted some peace and quiet, which was ironic considering the argument between his girlfriend and her friend, Tanya, was still playing out in the background.

And Facebook. Everyone was a friend, just six clicks away from everyone else. What was this modern urge to keep in touch?

There was a red phone box across the street, a lonely sentinel from a forgotten age when people met at the phone box as opposed to phoning each other to 'not meet'. Now it was a dumping ground for half-eaten takeaways.

He sighed and the choir of reflections sighed too before disappearing in the fog of condensation. Down there in the city streets, friends met, embraced, and continued talking to whoever was on the other end of their phone. No-one was actually *with* who they were with.

When he met someone in a bar, he was with that person – or, as now deadlocked behind the security of his front door, he was alone. Whereas, Shirley could sit opposite him in a restaurant, while all the time she was really with her oh-so-understanding friend somewhere else, forcing him to listen to half a conversation that occasionally alluded to her boyfriend, the silent partner sitting opposite. When he was allowed to speak, she went "uh-huh" and "hmmm" as she texted.

"Beeeeep! End of messages."

His sister had once had a Tamagotchi, and she had spent a long fortnight pressing the buttons to feed and nurture the plastic life-form. She'd developed the same look of vacant concentration that everyone had nowadays, as they texted to keep in touch with friends they didn't meet. Once, his sister had asked him to look after her Tamagotchi: it had died.

His old phone didn't work because he studiously didn't switch it on.

Now he had two phones (or three, or four counting the old mobile and the landline) and at least one woman to disappoint. He supposed that he could swap the SIM card between them depending on whether he was booked for a romantic evening or family meal, but he was bound to get that wrong.

Two: such choice, and where was the old one anyway?

He moved the two boxes aside, hunting behind and under. He liked things to be just right. A place for everything and everything in its place as his Aunt used to say. His flat was arranged neatly, just so, with strong lines and functional furniture; it was, dare he say it, masculine. He was a bachelor after all and it was important to get things right. That was the plan anyway. OK, so a lot of things were in the junk room, but they were junk and that was their place, and he wasn't 100% sure where the toolbox was, but everything he needed was in exactly-

"Shit!"

The cards fluttered down to the floor.

One of these gifts was from his mother and the other from his girlfriend, but now there was a real potential for farce as he couldn't tell which was from whom. He supposed he could work it out: which device would a mother purchase, which model would a girlfriend buy; but they both looked like products a salesman would recommend.

Perhaps he should just not bother, but he needed a girlfriend because a) he had to eat out with someone, and b) he wanted to sleep with someone. Probably his girlfriend's gift then - Mothers always loved you, they came free with being born.

Or perhaps he should just pick one, the best, and have 50% of the potential appreciation.

His old phone wasn't around. He could have sworn he'd put it on the Davenport. People were always misplacing their phones, weren't they?

Ring it! That was the trick.

A quick rip of cardboard – urg, something was a bit sticky – and a dumping of excess packaging meant that he had the two new phones arranged before him: bowl (keys and change), Phone A (silver), Phone B (black), paraphernalia of chargers and paperwork, desklight. Phone B flipped up and... what was his old mobile number? Oh, Seven, Seven, Something, Oh... there was a Four and an Eight. However, the new phones didn't work as they were still bereft of SIM card and mains juice.

Ring it with the landline.

What was his mobile number? Oh, Seven... Seven...

Where would he have written it down?

He opened the Davenport's drawer and rummaged through the old batteries, a pair of pliers (he had a toolbox somewhere), ruler, Euros, pens, pizza delivery coupons, ah ha! There was his collection of business cards with his name and numbers embossed in blue. Picking up the bulky handset, he stabbed Oh, Seven, Seven, Nine... held the receiver between his shoulder and head... just needed to move the rubber band aside to read the middle digits to enter those, and then, yep, there was an Eight and then a Four.

There was a distant chirp-chirp like some lost budgie and he walked nearer and nearer, homing in, until the phone cord became tight. He put it down on the floor and searched: warmer, warmer, colder, warmer, very w-

The sound stopped!

"Bollocks!"

Oh, the sodding thing had answered and was merrily recording his own swearing.

Back at the Davenport, he hung up, counted a non-calming ten and then pressed Redial: chirp-chirp, it went right through him as usual. He dashed to the lounge and then around the sofa to the coffee table and then to the other sofa and then back to the table because there was the little bugger hiding under the Radio Times.

"Gotcha!"

Bowl, paraphernalia, phone, desk light, old mobile, Phone A and Phone B.

He preferred his old phone. OK, it was old fashioned but it had lived in his pocket, or under the Radio Times or... wherever it was that phones went when you weren't looking, for a long time. It was U. N. blue, whereas the new phones were sleek in surgical steel or evil black.

It was a simple decision, check the features and pick the best one – logically.

The beer tasted good once he'd flipped the cap off, cold from the fridge and refreshing. He sat in the kitchen with the bumph from the new phones on the table. The booklets were expensively made for things that would be read once, if that, and then thrown away. It all added to the cost of the phones no doubt. By the time he'd skimmed through everything, his bottle was empty.

Maybe he should keep the cheap one and cash in the most expensive, but then he'd need the receipt.

"Eenie, meanie, miney... beer."

Another beer was a good idea.

Which one felt best in his pocket? That was worth considering.

Back at the Davenport, there was bowl, paraphernalia, phone, desklight, old mobile, Phone A and...

Phone B had gone. He looked under the Davenport – nope.

"Oh, for..."

OK, losing his usual phone was fair enough, because he didn't really care about it, but these ones were only just out of their packaging. It couldn't have run away, could it?

He must have picked it up and absently-mindedly put it down somewhere. Retrace your steps, he thought: kitchen, fridge, table...

There it was on the arm of the sofa.

He picked it up and realised then that he'd need a small screwdriver to open the old phone. He had a toolbox somewhere. In the kitchen he found a teaspoon and a small knife. One of these must do the trick and sure enough, once he was back at the Davenport, the end of the teaspoon prised it open. The SIM card cover clicked out. He really must sort out his tools, he thought, as he popped the spoon and knife into the Davenport's drawer next to the pliers.

So, old mobile, Phone A and... oh, for f- he'd had it in his hand not five seconds ago.

It wasn't under the Davenport or on the arm of the sofa.

He patted himself all over, but it wasn't in any pocket.

Something moved by the sofa.

A trick of the light?

No, it hadn't, it was a shadow from outside.

Or a rat.

Riiinng!

He nearly had a heart attack.

"Hello," his answering machine said, imitating him, "I'm not in at the moment, so if you'd like to leave a message, I'll get back to you."

"Hi, Keith, you've not, like, texted me with the new phone, so I don't know your new number. Text me. Love."

Beeeeep: "Thank you for calling."

Why did the stupid woman thank his callers *after they'd hung up!!!*

It could have been a rat. There was a rodent problem due to the local take-away, the half-eaten food dumped across the road, but surely not in his apartment. Vermin would have had to get past the lobby, up in the lift and then through his security door.

Best check.

He got down on his hands and knees, and then wondered what he'd do if he did find a rat. Perhaps he should get a hammer? He had a tool box somewhere: junk room.

Oh just look, you're a grown man.

He saw it: the missing phone.

There is was, under the sofa, about three inches away. Jeez - and beer was supposed to relax you. He shifted position and rammed his hand under up to his wrist. Moving side to side he tried to make contact, but he couldn't. All he could feel was the rough material on the underside of the sofa sawing away at his flesh. He took his hand out and had another look. It was there, lying calmly, and, now he looked properly, about six or seven inches away.

"Bloody typical!"

He found a ruler in the Davenport's drawer, and, after a final visual check, probed under the sofa with it: nothing.

"For goodness sake."

Practically upside-down, he found a position where he could look and probe with the ruler at the same time. Yep, the phone was over 12 inches/30 cm exactly and so irritatingly just too far away.

He went round the back, moved the sofa aside, which is what he should have done in the first place, and picked it up. Also under the sofa were a couple of beer bottle tops and the spare set of car keys, which had gone missing on-

"Fuck!"

He dropped the phone, it bounced. Like an after-shock, the image of the writhing legs and pincers processed through his brain.

"What the..."

The phone squirmed, limbs flailed, then one found enough leverage to flip it over, and then it scurried across the carpet to disappear again under the sofa.

He took a tiny step backwards almost to create a space between him and where the surprise had happened. After a quick glance at his hand, he wiped his fingers against his trousers even though they were dry.

There was some big... something in the phone, something big... with legs! And pincers!

Surely not?

He pushed the sofa aside with his foot. It was like turning a rock over when he saw the black object jerk and scuttle back under for safety.

Suddenly, he found himself standing on the sofa squealing like a little girl.

What the fuck was that!?

He stepped back and forth on the comfy seat, wondering what to do next, when the thing crawled out from under the sofa and scampered across the lounge towards the hallway.

"Hello," he heard his own voice say, "I'm not in at the moment, so if you'd like to leave a message, I'll get back to you."

He leapt off the sofa, tugged in both directions by a desire to attack and a fear of getting close, and stumbled as he landed on the carpet. The creature turned the corner and he was in pursuit, coming to an abrupt stop when he saw the mobile phone clawing its way up the Davenport's table leg.

The repulsive thing heaved itself onto the surface, and then shook its shell-like, sleek plastic casing off. It pulsed as it breathed, gasping with the effort of wriggling across. It reached his old mobile phone, touched and pawed at the case to ease it open. Folding and collapsing, it turned, backed in and squeezed itself inside.

There was just the bowl, paraphernalia, phone, desk light, Phone A (Silver), Phone B (Black), which was on its side, glistening slightly where the slime trail across the Davenport started, and... his old mobile lying there as if there was nothing the matter.

He snatched up a guarantee card from all the bumph and used it to poke his old mobile – nothing. He tried again, nothing, and again, noth- suddenly it moved, legs appeared and it scurried to the edge. He hit it with the card, which did nothing but waft the air, so he hefted the landline to attack. The creature jumped away, sprang into the air.

Instinctively, he grabbed the mobile phone it had come from and flung it at the creature as it landed. He missed. The projectile caught the skirting board and exploded into pieces, screen, buttons, battery, all flying in ballistic trajectories.

Still holding the heavy landline aloft, he advanced.

It knew: it looked at him with its single glassy Cyclops eye and it backed away along the hallway until he had the little bugger cowering in the corner.

"Here boy, here boy," he said sweetly.

He raised the Bakelite weapon and swung forward, but it stopped dead, checked mid-air as it reached the end of its tether, the cord was as a straight black line marked the shortest distance between phone and socket. He twisted it, yanked and the jack failed at the phone socket with a loud plastic crack. The creature seized its chance and crabbed over his left foot. He jerked away with a deep seated phobic response, dropping the phone as he did so: it rang as it bounced badly. The thing disappeared again under the sofa.

"Right!"

Anger made him brave. He stormed over, bumped the sofa to one side and grabbed it in one single, deft movement. He had it. It wriggled, it writhed, pincers clipped around, but he ignored this. In the kitchen, he whipped out one of the expensive, unused kitchen knives from its holder, and just stopped himself from stabbing it. It wasn't a good idea to do that while he was holding it in his hand.

"OK!"

Carefully, he planned what he was going to do, and then: he dropped it on its back in the middle of the kitchen table and stabbed it in one decisive action. The knife went sharply through its writhing body as it was trying to right itself. The point jabbed in and when he drew back for another lunge, it was still impaled on the blade. He rammed down again - hard - burying the stainless steel into the tabletop. The knife oscillated like a tuning fork when he let go.

Pinned, the creature flailed desperately.

He watched it for a long time after it had died, its innards oozing dark goo across the polishing surface, until he was absolutely sure. His heart still pounded away. He felt sick. When he opened the fridge to get a beer, the cold antiseptic light fell in a strip across the dead monstrosity. The fizz of the beer made him choke.

He needed someone to talk to, anyone: Shirley, his Mum. He needed his Mum.

The landline was lying on the hallway floor where he'd dropped it. It was dead, then he remembered that the line had been yanked out of the socket. He tried putting it back, but the plastic had distorted when it had snapped.

Then he remembered the second new phone, the silver one, but that probably didn't have a SIM card either. He could try and recover his old SIM card from the possessed and damaged black phone, but he didn't fancy that idea at all. Even the thought of going back into the kitchen made him shudder. He looked at the kitchen door.

Putting it off for as long as possible, he went to find the silver phone, but that wasn't on the Davenport. Clearly it had been knocked off during the struggle, so, looking round, he... there was the phone box opposite. He didn't have to face the creature again after all.

His keys were in the bowl, and he dashed out without a jacket feeling the bite of the cold night. It was refreshing, cleansing even. There were passers-by, all involved with conversations elsewhere, and he felt a revulsion - what if...

There was a minefield of discarded takeaways to negotiate, and then he was in the old phone box with the heavy door closing behind him. The cubicle smelt of urine. He tapped the number accurately, remembering the change of code since he had first learnt it by heart when he'd been a little boy. There was no answer, there was no sound at all, and, after banging the metal hook several times, he discovered that the cord to the receiver had been vandalised.

There was still the other mobile phone; perhaps, against all odds, it came with a SIM and credit – worth a try.

He waited for a gap in the stream of passers-by, all walking like zombies with a hand held tight to the side of their heads, and all oblivious to the distress of a fellow human being.

Once back in the centrally heated warmth of his flat, he found the other new mobile, all bright and shiny, under the Davenport.

He flipped it over and opened the SIM slot – of course it didn't come with a SIM.

He pushed the kitchen door open with his toe and peered in. The knife was still stuck in the kitchen table, still stabbed through the creature's corpse. Revolted, but determined, he crept closer. It didn't move.

There was nothing else for it, so he took hold of the handle with both hands and pulled. On the second jerk, it came out from the polished wood. The thing was like meat struck on a skewer and its legs and pincers hung, loose and disjointed like a puppet with its strings cut. Careful not to touch anything organic, he used his fingernail to ease the slider open and drop the SIM card out. It landed, miraculously intact.

He wondered what to do with the dead – whatever. He should report it, or sell it on e-bay... or better still the News might pay for a picture? He had a positive glut of available cameras if he included his two new... one new phone.

Back in the hallway, he tried to put the SIM card into the new phone, but it wouldn't go: he tried this way, that way - bloody damn stupid. He found the correct procedure in the second manual he tried. You had to push the battery back. Finally it went in, closed and powered up. Thank God.

All his contacts were there: 'M' came before 'S', so he green buttoned his Mother.

It rang – please pick up, pick up, pick up, pick-

"Mum, you're not going to beli.... it's Keith... Keith, your son... look-"

The phone vibrated in his hand as if a text was coming through on silent. Several pincers shot out to grip his face and ear, and there was a suction, a slurping adhesion as the phone clamped itself to his skin and needled into his flesh with an excruciating tickling caused by all the legs, claws and tentacles.

"Christ!"

His mother's voice sounded through the speaker, distant,

distorted by the pulsing underwater whoosh.

He brought his left hand around to assist his right. There had been one of those things in both phones. He had to get the bloody thing off and-

Something slithered out, pumped into his ear like a tube inserting itself, pulsing as it squeezed out its contents. The pressure built, a deep roaring of a sea, followed by a blissful pop! as it penetrated his ear drum. This wonderful release was punctured by a searing pain that gifted him the super-human strength to tear the creature off and fling it across the room. It crashed off the coffee table and bounced to land, legs up, on the carpet. A few spasms later, the thing died with a squirting ejection of goo.

"Fuck, fuck!"

The side of his face was wet with fresh blood, and he stabbed and searched with his fingers for the object forced inside the delicate tunnels of his ear. He heard a rasping, harmonic blare as it scrunched up his auditory canal. When it touched his cochlea, all balance went and he toppled over like a drunk on a pitching boat. He lay there paralysed, eyes blindly wide, as a prickling sensation spread within his skull.

Gradually the man's breathing settled as the explosive need for oxygen decayed. Time ceased to have meaning. The digital bars of the clock meant nothing; they were random, changing as they felt like it with as much significance as the light and dark that came through the triple-glazed window.

Eventually, creating a new flow of soothing warm blood over the long caked and dried stains across the man's face, a new life p- p- pus- pushed and pop! It emerged, air rushing into its internal tubes and sacs as it faltered, then fell from the man's unshaven face. Its brand new body glistened and bent impossibly as its legs pulled it across the rough carpet.

Another set of legs emerged from the man's ear like the waving stamens in a beautiful flower. Before it had pulled itself free, another was following, and another. And another. Soon, a long line of misshapen creatures, none truly squid, or crab, or spider, followed each other along trails of foetal fluid.

Two found the waiting mobile phone, and fought each other for it.

A third creature bypassed them.

Painfully, it gripped its dead parent and pulled the crumbling form from the phone casing. The desiccated corpse shattered into dust. The new offspring turned round and backed into the phone, its body finding a new shape in the rectangular cavities as if it was a paste. Once inside its newly acquired armoured shell, it turned to fight off its vulnerable unprotected brothers and sisters. The battle was short. Soon there was only the phone and the ruptured remains of the rest of the brood.

The phone rang: a trill, insistent noise, and so the man got up and talked to it: there, there, the man said, as he gently put it to his ear, so the hatchling could feed.

Once it was gorged, the man put it down carefully, and set about tidying away the mess, flicking the detritus into the pedal bin with a dust pan and brush, before returning to the phone. The man sat with the cooing creature, tickled its underside and massaged the baby through the buttons. It chirped happily, and everything was right with the world.

Soon, the man would take it for a walk. They could go to the shops together. There would be new phones there, bright and shiny, and each would make such a perfect present for all his friends and then they could all keep in touch.

DANIEL WILKES is an undergraduate BA Hons English student, researching post-communist propagandist writing in his own time; he also writes short stories, poetry and satire. He's a reader of surrealism, science fiction and modern American literature and post-war poetry.

The Bucket Hunt
by Daniel Wilkes

-*Git the fuckin' buckit.* C***'s shrill bark begins a frenetic scampering of blind eyes, hands and feet. Two collide with a muffled squeal, a third falls onto the pile. It is safer to be still so I stay lounged against the damp wall in silence, head tilted to the grunts a few feet ahead. *Another* falls over the messy orgy, bouncing me out of comfort. –*ARHH GOH IY,* dribbles out of a lazy mouth, somewhere to my left. A fleeting round of applause from above concludes The Bucket Hunt.

A knuckle-on-knuckle carousel played by her stilettos on the metal staircase is augmented by the offbeat CHING! of the chain that follows her lead. My ring twinkles with childhood excitement – I have been out of favour for a while now, but it could always be your turn. The knuckles stop, the chain follows suit. –*You're a pretty one.* I feel the loud crack of a gloved hand across the room. C*** giggles innocently at the sound of her own venom. I hear her fondle the chain and clip it to the neck of one in the clumsy pile of others ahead. A few tugs and she stiletto-steps back up the stairwell, stalked by a panting mouth. The door is pulled shut behind her by Finney, one of The Select. I count the three bolts-

Dun...
Kah-Dun...
Dun.

And here I am again. Left to stew in C***'s pit for that while longer.

The three minutes after The Bucket Hunt always feel like my Elysian Fields– lying naked in a blanket of sweat, holding my cock in my left hand, the right groping for flesh in the baroque silence. Down here you get real silence. And in silence, everything stops. Time decays, and the smallest spank from the smallest hand matches your best blowjob. In the dark everybody is different, even nature.

* * *

Joanne sleeps well, I don't. It is easier to sleep here. Outside the pit I never sleep. An old Chinaman taught me how to slip between; he gave me an ekaggata, a jade statue of a woman. He taught me to focus upon a single point until my body and mind attuned. Her nipple teased the crease of her kimono to a pyramidic point. I named her Sally.

* * *

We are fed daily. Healthy portions of red meat are dished out at each meal with a glass bottle of milk. –It helps maintain erections and a steady supply of sperm. Keeps them keen too, C*** regularly informs The Select. *Some-other* put one up his arse base first while *Another* pissed into the bottleneck. Finney smashed it with a bat. I never saw them again. Dirty fuckers.

* * *

DO YOU LOVE ME?... LIKE I LOVE YOU?

Chhhh-Wuk-Wuk-Chhhhh! C*** whipped along with the Bad Seeds, lording over me on the bed. I am tied face-down into a floral bedspread. Out of the corner of my eye I see others masturbating onto a human-shaped tarpaulin tortilla. Her lashes keep up to an impressive tempo, she plays bass drum with her knuckle-stiletto, jabbing at my peachy bum cheek. – *WAAAUHHHH,* she wails along with Nick Cave whilst pounding my back.

I don't know how long I have been here. It could have been 4 hours or 52 seconds, I don't care.

The whip stops. My moan is echoed by *Somebody* jaffing onto the salty iron maiden. I hear Velcro being jawed apart. The tear twists my neck to attention. A mercury-blonde career woman sprouts from the Velcro labia all doe-eyed and twitchy. C*** lies down on my back – skin on skin. Her perky tits fill the curve of my back. She bites my earlobe and draws blood. With one hand she offers me a swig of Redbull, whilst the other goes to town on my arsehole. She tosses the can aside and reaches around for my cock. Finney, in his gimp mask, cuts the ties; I fall limp into the bed. C*** turns me over and slips on top.

* * *

I wake up in a comforting room in pinstriped pajamas. The window is ajar and the British summer frolics with the suburbs of Birmingham. A soft rap at the door and Finney walks in wearing a virgin-white polo tucked into his light brown slacks. – *Mr. Busby. I 'ope your stay has been enjoyable.* I nod. Finney's accent is weak, only the odd word is peppered with a brummie drawl. –*We have a conservative approwach to business. Your clawuthes are in the ambruy.* He gestures to a cheap, wooden wardrobe in the corner. –*W've taken the payment from your accowunt under a charituy.* He gives a snappy smile and stands up. –*You can see yourself out.* He closes the door. *Zzzzzzp.* I hear the zip of Finney's leather gimp mask. It is followed by eager footsteps.

* * *

I call a taxi from my iPhone before getting dressed. My hair, face, skin, all look clean. Even the dirt under my nails is gone. My teeth could stun a passing bird in the right light. *Bzzzzz... Bzzzzzz.* I check my text and reply:

Carol (PA)
Don't forget Joanne's birthday present. <

Me
> http://en.bulgari.com/productDetail.jsp?prod=OR853430, get it delivered. Treat yourself too x

Carol (PA)
Thanks. x <

I leave the room to meet the taxi outside. I pass a signed picture of Lenny Henry holding C*** by the waist in the hallway. The door closest to the stairs bounces to a neat Bonhamesque rhythm, met by the wails of a woman at her peak. I play with my tie in front of the mirror by the door, straighten my lapel and head out into the light.

SUZANNE WRIGHT'S first novel, *The Love Child's Mother*, was published after she retired from teaching. It is about adoption and reunion, and draws on her experience as a birth mother in the 1960s. She has also written a number of short stories and poems, and a play to be performed next year at the Birmingham Drama Festival. Currently, she is working on her second novel.

Collision
by Suzanne Wright

Fucking tourists!

Mehmet mentally practised his new adjective, one of the many things he'd learned from the clients in his first season as a tour guide.

Of course he'd never say it out loud.

Twenty eight of these tourists waited patiently on the coach by the mosque in Ovacik for the remaining six of the group to show up, so they could begin the trip to the carpet co-operative, Saklikent Gorge, the hill tombs of Tlos, for lunch at the trout farm and finally a walk round the 'Ghost Village' of Kayakoy.

Not a word of apology when they arrived, all together. They shuffled down the aisle of the bus, men with beer bellies, women in shorts and t-shirts revealing every detail of aging and unattractive bodies. At first he'd been shocked at such immodesty, but that was three months ago.

The last person, a bulky older woman with red hair and flowered shorts, brushed against him as she passed, and knocked the clip-board from his hands.

"Och, sorry hinny," she said without a trace of remorse and hardly a backward glance. Her breath smelled strange. Whiskey. And it was only 10am.

He checked the names of his passengers against his list. The red head, he noticed, was Jane Brolan.

A brief word with Mohammed, his driver, and the excursion began. Mehmet picked up the microphone and began his charm offensive with some information about himself, his education, the Turkish university system, his home village in the mountains and some of the local customs.

"In my village a single woman who wants to be married leaves an empty glass bottle on the window sill. If a man breaks it, he has to marry her. If you break it by accident you still have to marry her. When a man wants to marry he goes to see the parents and if they agree, he can marry. If not, they can elope. But if the girl is under eighteen – you go to jail. Jail is ok in Turkey, you know, it's air conditioned and has a jacuzzi."

All the tourists - English, Scottish, German and two Russians - laughed.

They liked him.

The coach passed through the immaculate empty villas and apartments of the outer fringes of Fethiye: the inner fringes of older apartment blocks with balconies festooned with drying laundry and plants: the inner core of scruffy shops, broken pavements and empty spaces full of rubbish: and finally the glamour of the modern centre. He chatted and joked, teaching them Turkish phrases, telling stories.

"In Turkey, in history, we have war with the Greeks. This is our custom. Right now, the Greeks have no money so there is no war. Later, when they have money, and they can afford it, we fight them again."

They laughed. They loved him.

At the carpet co-operative - wonderful. Two of them bought carpets, giving him a little commission. They were impressed by the Saklikent Gorge, and many of them returned to the coach wet from paddling in the icy waters.

The first hint of trouble began as the Mercedes coach began the ascent of the Taurus mountains en route to Tlos and the trout farm. The road zigzagged ever more steeply and the hydraulic system began hissing, gears grinding. The coach slowed to a crawl, stopped, crawled on. On one side of the road lay a breathtaking drop to the vast alluvial plain with its silver thread of river which swept between the surrounding mountains down to the sea; on the other side olive trees clung to steep rock.

The passengers barely noticed the engine noise, assuming this was normal on such a steep gradient, confident that the driver had done this journey many times before.

Mohammed was a skinny man with no front teeth, a sweet and unassuming man, and his dark eyes with yellow whites showed apprehension. It was early October and he and Mehmet both knew that the coach was overdue for a service. It was soon to be scrapped and the boss wasn't about to spend his profits on spare parts at this point in the season. Mohammed pulled to a halt then tried first gear again. Passengers began to mutter.

They rounded another tight bend. A fast flowing stream, tumbling down the mountainside and diving under the curve, had taken a bite from the crumbling tarmac on the down side. One orange cone stood as a hazard warning.

Across the valley appeared the ancient Lycian hill tombs of Tlos, carved into the rock face, their doors and windows gaping in the heat like eye sockets. Above the tombs a ragged Turkish flag flapped in the stifling breeze.

The coach shuddered on, slowed, groaned and slid back towards the edge of the road above the bend.

Jane Brolan, sitting on her own by the side exit, craned to see backwards. From her perspective the coach probably appeared to be suspended over the steep drop. She gasped, then screamed.

"Let me offa this cooch."

Her evident panic spread perceptibly to the other passengers. Many of them left their seats to view the danger for themselves.

"Please keep to your seats," Mehmet urged, fearful that so much weight on one side might just unbalance the coach, causing even more difficulties.

Mohammed switched off the air conditioning, using all the power available to pull forward. The coach lurched further up the narrow road, but finally shuddered to a halt.

Mehmet phoned his boss and simultaneously consulted Mohammed. The side door hissed open and Mehmet stepped out onto the strip of tarmac between the coach and the edge of the road and walked back, past the hot oily air pumping out from the engine, to the bend to assess the situation.

The air was fresh above the stream. Mehmet heard a bird chirp, drowsy in the afternoon heat, and olive leaves rustled in the breeze. The water gurgled happily, romping away into the under growth, a source of inexhaustible energy. He looked back at the coach, like a stranded whale on the mountain road, and wished he didn't have to go back. He had no idea what to do next. Basically, the coach was knackered, and in an unmanoeuvrable position.

An expectant hush greeted his return.

Without the air conditioning, even with the door open, the temperature in the coach was rising rapidly. Ignoring the passengers he went to get Mohammed who cut the engine and followed him to the side exit.

"My God, they're leaving us alone on the coach. We'll all be killed," Jane Brolan said loudly as they descended the steps under her gaze. The other passengers muttered uneasily. Mehmet pretended he hadn't heard her.

They stood together on the hot tarmac, Mehmet on the phone to his boss, Mohammed on his phone speaking to the mechanic, and they formed a plan.

Mohammed returned to his seat. He switched on the engine, located Mehmet in the rear view mirrors, and followed his beckoning hands back, back, away from the edge, and into the curve, until the bumper scraped against the rock face and the length of the coach blocked both narrow lanes across the bend. The passengers could surely hear the gurgling water below the wheels. Mehmet half expected them to abandon the coach, and guessed that only fear kept them in their seats. That, plus their predisposition to do as they were told and trust the driver. Cars on both sides waited to pass, tooting, edging forward. One tried to squeeze between the coach and the orange cone then reversed back.

Miraculously, inch by inch, Mehmet guided the driver safely past the bend. To the passengers it must often have appeared that the coach was about to tumble down the mountainside, but eventually it came to rest on the straight, opposite a small roadside stall.

Mehmet dreaded the next task, but had no choice. He stepped back onto the coach and picked up the microphone. The muttering faded to silence. Avoiding the eye of his fat tormentor and trying to keep his voice even, he said, 'Ladies and gentlemen, we must get off and wait for another coach which will be here in two minutes. Please kindly wait in the shade of the trees by the stall.'

Now safe, the passengers gave vent to their anxiety, though none so angrily as the big woman. He didn't understand her words, the accent was unfamiliar, though he did realise that many of them were variations on 'fuck'. What was this obsession they had with 'fuck'?

He stood ready to help people off the last step which was a little rickety. As her flowered shorts and mottled thighs appeared at the top of the steps he prayed that the bottom step would hold. Her slab of a foot with fat sausage toes slammed into the dodgy step which shook, but held firm. She ignored his proffered hand.

"Ah've jest aboot had a sken foo," she snarled incomprehensibly. "And where, may Ah ask, are you going to get a cooch on a mountain top in two minutes?" She stomped off, red and sweating, into the shade of the olive trees by the stall.

He had in fact arranged that another coach which had already delivered its passengers to the trout farm, ten minutes away, was coming to pick them up, but he didn't have chance to explain.

The owner of the stall, respectable in headscarf and long sleeves, who reminded him of his Aunt Zia, watched in amazement as the coach disgorged its passengers, then realised she was facing her best sales opportunity for weeks, and began to sell; beads, scarves, jewellery, everything. It kept some of the women amused while they waited in the heat.

The passengers were clearly surprised to see a replacement coach arrive so quickly, though it made no difference to Brolan's surly mood.

After a much shortened visit to the tombs, starving, they reached the trout farm for lunch well after 3.0 pm. The herd of hungry tourists was not a pretty sight, especially when so many of them, judging by their size, were clearly used to eating much and often.

The mood of the tight queue round the buffet table was not happy. Small plates were heaped high. The last half dozen people found that several of the food containers were empty, including the roast potatoes. And one of these people was – his personal tormentor in the flowered shorts. He could see her face, hear her voice. He went and hid in the shrubs by the trout stream, and smoked three Marlboro in quick succession.

You could put their lives in danger, it seemed, and they'd accept it, but take away their roast potatoes and you would never be forgiven.

He managed to remain hidden until his passengers began to return to the coach after lunch when he was forced to emerge. Several people expressed their discontent, some quite forcefully. Jane Brolan shouldered her way through the crowd, her voice strident. Her words, words which should never pass the lips of a female, singed his heart, this morning as light and free as the birds in the sky. Her mouth twisted into an ugly vicious sneer as she sliced into his spirit, cutting and shredding his confidence. The more angry she became, the stronger her accent and the less he understood the actual words. Finally she stopped and got back onto the coach.

The microphone remained in its stand on the return journey, as Mehmet's ability to charm the passengers had now completely evaporated. His self esteem in shreds, all adult dignity gone, he knew that one more word from Brolan and he would cry.

It was with profound relief that he saw the last tourist off the bus in Ovacik.

When he'd finished and handed over the coach, instead of heading for his room, and evening meal, he decided to walk along the back lanes of the village, by the cemetery. He needed to turn over the events of the day and figure out how else he could have handled them.

Dust and insects floated on the slanting rays of the late afternoon sun. The blue arch of the sky changed second by second to the Turkish delight colours of sunset. Quickly the horizon beyond the mosque turned to fire. Stirred by the nasal wail of the muezzin, flocks of birds swirled like tea leaves in a crimson brew. A hard white moon, almost full, hung above the mountains, bathing the lane in silver light which soaked away into the ragged trees of the cemetery. Moths flittered in crisp yellow weeds and, beyond the wall, light glimmered on white graves set between twisting tree trunks. A city of the dead, waiting for eternity.

On the other side of the lane stood a Lego town of new palaces, white, cream and darker cream, equally silent, even more empty. Lights showed in only two or three. Moonlight reflected on dark oblong swimming pools. All waited to be recalled to life by their absent owners.

Finally the muezzin ceased.

Far away a dog barked. A cock crowed.

Mehmet's footsteps barely disturbed the velvet dusk as he trod the lane, the one living creature between the two worlds of ghosts.

The villas gleamed like giant mausoleums. Only two years ago that was a field where sheep and goats grazed the stony ground under the olive trees, opposite the sanctuary of the departed. Now their blank windows overlooked the holy resting places of those who sought ever lasting peace and solitude. The traditional ways of grace and respect were pushed aside to accommodate the ugliness and lack of dignity of the strangers from cold places who sought the sunshine and warmth but brought their coldness and harshness of life with them.

Burdened by his thoughts, he failed to notice the figure approaching from the other end of the lane. He reached a gap in the trees and emerged from the cool shadows into the moonlight.... and came face to face with the woman, Jane fucking Brolan, as if he had summoned her presence by the power of his despair.

He halted, embarrassed.

She startled: "Jesus Christ!"

Breath rattled in her throat as if an elephant was sitting on her chest. The air between them was thick, filled with rushing and throbbing. Bats thrashed above the trees. Her hands pressed into her chest. She stumbled and crumpled, a lead weight, onto her knees and did not seem to feel the sharp pebbles. She tipped forward and did not move.

Mehmet gazed at the lumpen form at his feet, frozen with shock. Her breath came in irregular shuddering gurgles.

What should he do? He could not lay hands on this woman. Her anger terrified him. Leave her there? Pretend he had not seen her? Let her breathe her last?

Her handbag had spilled its contents. He knelt to push them back and caught the hot feral smell of her body. The passport lay open. The photograph was clear, and it showed that the woman was James Brolan, a man, aged fifty two. Confusion crowded out every rational thought, every fear, every last trace of the events of the afternoon. His thoughts darted here and there, trying to fit this new information into some pattern he could understand, something which would chime with his previous experience of life and give some indication of how to respond and make sense of the situation. What should he do?

Mehmet lifted his eyes to where the mosque minaret, nestled in its curved domes, stood tall and erect, pointing to the eternity of the next world. Reluctantly he returned his gaze to the figure at his feet. He, or she, was not ready to make that journey, especially not dressed like that, and would not have had to but for his own sudden appearance.

Overcoming his fear, Mohammed pulled the heavy body into the recovery position. He took out his phone and dialled 156. Then he ran to the nearest villa which showed lights and hammered on the door.